Corker

A NOVEL BY ANYA BATEMAN

BOOKCRAFT • SALT LAKE CITY, UTAH

Library of Congress Catalog Card Number: 81-71439
ISBN 0-88494-448-4

First Printing, 1982

Lithographed in the United States of America
PUBLISHERS PRESS
Salt Lake City, Utah

1

"Steve, old buddy, is that you?" I called out, as I headed down our driveway toward the Morgans' back yard. I was almost certain it had been my best friend's voice I had just heard.

"Ben?" Sure enough, it had been his voice, because Steve appeared from behind the Morgans' van, carrying his towheaded younger brother on his shoulders. I knew I had to pull my act together quickly, and I grinned widely, adopted a Western stance, and drawled: "You the dude they call the Missionary Kid? They call me Ben—Big Bad Ben, toughest cowpoke in these here parts." It was a line from an old roadshow, and we had often kidded about it before his mission.

Steve remembered. He quickly lowered Joshua, leaned back with his thumbs in his pockets, and drawled, "Reckon that's a challenge, cowboy." Then he hurried toward me and grabbed my hand with a right that almost knocked me over.

"Hey, none of this handshaking stuff!" I objected. "You're a civilian now. Give me ten!"

He slapped both my hands, and I returned the favor. It was so good to see him that I had to swallow to get control. I didn't feel so bad, though, when I noticed Steve's eyes were slightly moist.

"It's mighty good to see you," he said.

I hit him in the stomach. "Well, it's mighty good to see you, you know that? Let me look at you."

I stood back. Steve looked clean and lean, and the good humor still filtered through his eyes. "I should have guessed. You haven't changed. Hey, my next question is, Why did they release you early? We had a big party planned and a banner. What did you do—try to hold hands with a lady missionary?"

"Glad *you* haven't changed," Steve said, smiling.

"Did they let you go because of that airline strike that might be coming up?" I asked.

Steve nodded without much enthusiasm.

"You're not disappointed to get out early are you?"

"Oh, a little. I'm officially released now and everything's okay, but technically I still had a few more days."

Steve was sounding just like himself. It was exactly the kind of thing you could expect him to say. "Well, maybe you can make it up," I suggested. "You could tract the neighborhood and leave pamphlets."

"That's not a bad idea," Steve said thoughtfully, with mock seriousness. "How about going with me? We could start at your house." I knew Steve was talking about Corker, and I nodded, half-grinned, and changed the subject.

"How did you stay so trim? You make me feel like the Pillsbury doughboy. Look at this." I grabbed the extra flesh around my middle. "Your old buddy is getting fat. Eating comes too easily for me. I think it's my special talent."

Steve, polite as usual, only glanced at my bulging midriff and didn't express astonishment at my increase in weight. "Are you still chef over there?" he asked instead.

"Well, let me put it this way. If I want to get anything decent to eat, I have to cook. My mother hasn't stepped foot in a kitchen for five and a half years now, and Corker—well I don't let her near the kitchen since she tried to poison me."

Steve chuckled, but I noticed he had begun flushing slightly at the mention of Corker's name. He sat down in a lawn chair, lifting Joshua to his knee. "How is your kid sister, anyway?" he asked, trying to sound casual. It wasn't subtle of him to ask about her right away.

I hesitated. "Well, let's put it this way. Corker takes herself very seriously."

"She always did, didn't she?"

"More so now." I didn't know how to tell him that Corker, still intent on becoming a superwoman, was now concentrating on the "woman of steel" aspect of superwomanhood. There was a new hardness about her. I decided not to mention it. "She still checks off her goals with a sharp pencil," I said instead. "I guess you heard she just graduated." I tried to hide the misery in my voice.

"Her last letter mentioned that, or at least her last letter mentioned that that was her plan." He shook his head. "I don't know how she did it so fast."

I sighed. "Oh, you know my sister. She can do anything! Her middle name is Follow-through. When she sets a goal, she does it." I was a little bitter about Corker's graduation. I had planned to graduate first. I thought that would be appropriate, since I am three years older than Corker. But at the last I had changed majors again; and I hadn't made up some incompletes. And trying to get through college on five to seven hours a quarter is a slow process.

"Of course," I explained, "you've got to remember she just took a bunch of Mickey Mouse classes in fashion and dance." I wondered if that sounded as "sour grapes" to him as it did to me.

Steve pretended I hadn't said it. "You've got to hand it to her," he said.

"I suppose so."

Empathetic as usual, he slapped me on the back. I was becoming eager to change the subject, and I yawned. Talking about Corker always made me tired. It was the same story whenever Mother brought up the subject, which she had been doing too often lately. She was concerned about Corker's future. "We're losing her," she said. "She's just got to settle down and quit thinking about being big time."

"If grandchildren are what you have in mind, don't count on it," I answered. My mother had stared at me as if I had just broken her heart into tiny pieces and stepped on them.

I looked at Steve and wondered if he might be the answer to my mother's prayers. If anything, Steve seemed even more at peace with himself than ever. I knew him well enough to know that underneath his calm exterior he was strong and energetic and achievement-oriented. Steve was the kind of person who could accomplish with seemingly little effort. And he matched Corker in his output. Besides that, it was obvious his feelings for Corker were still intact. I was also pretty sure that Steve would be good for my sister. He had always had a way of touching a gentle vein in her. *But,* I asked myself as I watched him smiling at his little brother with genuine affection, *would Corker be good for Steve? That is the question.* I didn't want to think about it any more, and I changed the subject.

"And how was it? Is a mission all it's chalked up to be?"

Steve's blue eyes registered amusement. "You won't like my answer."

"Oh, oh! Best two years of your life?"

"Best two years of my life," he repeated, nodding.

"Why did I know you'd say that?"

He laughed. "I was never going to say it, but now I'm saying it." Then he added seriously. "Maybe because it really was. I've got to tell you about it. There's a lot to catch up on."

Joshua, eager for attention and becoming bored, was flipping his bottom lip against his teeth. I ruffled his hair. "Hey, guy, I guess you don't need old Ben any more now that big brother is home, huh? Guess I'll just be left out in the cold."

Joshua tried to look at my face, but I had lowered my head. "We can still be buddies, Big Ben," he said, with compassionate concern. "Course, I gotta like Steve best because he's my brother, but I can like you almost best."

"Oh, well, that's sure good news." I looked at Steve, and we chuckled at Joshua's tactful honesty. Joshua looked at me and then at Steve with puzzlement, and I couldn't help tickling him. That got him going, and suddenly he was batting at me.

"Hey, hold it down!" Steve said, trying to control Joshua's flailing arms.

"I like to hit him in the fat stomach," Joshua said, still struggling to reach me.

I stopped laughing. Joshua's charm was suddenly wavering. In fact, it was tottering on the brink, and I winced. "Gain a few pounds and the world is on your back," I muttered.

At the word *back*, Joshua began climbing on mine. "Gimme a piggy-back ride, Big Ben."

"Uh-uh! Get off my back." But he had wrapped his arms tightly around my neck and wouldn't let go. I got up slowly with a moan. "I'm too old for this sort of thing."

"Giddy-up," Joshua jerked, and I groaned. I may have looked like the average piggy giving a piggy-back ride, but by the time I got to the end of the driveway I was sounding more like the Big Bad Wolf. I was huffing and puffing under the strain of Joshua's forty pounds.

"I'm just a little out of shape," I complained, as I galloped back to my lawn chair and plopped into it with a sigh.

It was at that moment that Darlene, Steve's leggy sister, came sprinting home from her early morning jogging. Darlene had just turned eighteen, and she looked like the goddess of good health. Her golden skin matched the light streaks in her brown hair. Seeing Darlene made me self-conscious about my breathless condition, but also didn't help it any.

"How did you do?" Steve asked.

"Three miles." She flicked away a drop of perspiration from her forehead with a delicate index finger. Darlene could even make sweating look feminine.

"Three miles, huh?" I repeated. "Not bad."

"Not bad? That's terrific," Steve said, with admiration in his voice.

"That's what I said. Not bad at all." I waited for Darlene to look at me with her light blue eyes, the Morgan trademark, but she only beamed at Steve and then walked over to the far end of the yard to check the tomatoes before she went into the house, letting the screen door slam. "Guess you had a hard time recognizing some of your own kin, huh?" I said, still looking at the screen door.

"I hardly recognized this little guy." Steve was referring to Joshua, who was chasing a grasshopper and looking like a grasshopper himself in the process. "And the girls have really changed too."

"Yes," I agreed quickly. "Haven't they!" To my delight the Morgan girls were growing up and doing it nicely.

It's no wonder, I thought, as Frances, the matriarch of the Morgan clan, came out of the back door, wiping her hands on a towel that was attached to her floral apron. Even with a few curlers in her hair, Frances looked pleasant. She was one of those Mormon women they should write poems about, because she loved her job and it showed in her face. Frances was not only beautiful but amazing. She was Primary president; a great hostess; a good housekeeper who kept her home in tip-top shape, but comfortable; and, yes, she even baked bread. *And,* she was a devoted mother of seven. She was one of those women who makes other women nervous. It was too bad, because Frances was simply enjoying herself.

But I had observed Frances long enough to know that she wasn't quite perfect. Once I had seen her chasing Joshua for almost a half block after he had picked all the petunias she had just planted. She was shouting, "You'd better run faster! Run faster, you little stinker! Run like the dickens, because if I catch you, I'm going to clobber you!"

And when the back door was open, I sometimes heard her complaining, "Why am I the only one who ever picks up anything around here? Why?"

No, Frances wasn't perfect, but the fact that she was a little human didn't make anyone like her less.

Now an extra dose of love light was radiating from her as she looked at her oldest son. "I get the impression you're glad to have him back," I said.

"You betcha," she answered. "I just want to hug him all the time, but my kids have always been mean to me that way. They only let me hug them once in a while." She turned to Steve. "Want some breakfast? We're having pancakes."

I pictured Frances's golden pancakes with melted butter and thick gooey syrup. Frances seemed to read my mind. "Ben, there are a couple of pancakes in there with your name on them," she said.

"No kidding?" I got up quickly. "Could I see?"

As Steve and I followed his mother to the porch, I noticed that some of her seemed to be missing. "What are you trying to do, Frances, turn into one of those narrow-hipped models? You're fading away."

She giggled happily. "I'll tell you. Wanda, Phyllis and I are taking Corker's aerobics dance class and I've never had so much fun!"

"Don't tell me you've fallen prey to that hypnotizing music too." It seemed that half the women in the stake were taking Corker's aerobics dance class. The other half were taking her fashion and grooming classes, and she had a waiting list three pages long.

"It *is* habit-forming," Frances admitted. "But it's the good kind of habit-forming. I've never felt better in my life. That sister of yours, well, we've just got to keep her home, and that's all there is to it. She keeps talking about New York, but we're all working on keeping her here."

"Is she still talking about New York?" Steve asked quickly, as he held the screen door for us. "I'll have to talk her out of that."

Frances and I raised our eyebrows at each other. Then Frances smiled gently. *Not me!* I frowned with real concern for my buddy. *Good luck, Steve,* I thought, *because you'll need it.*

Corker was eating Cheerios and reading *Working Woman* when I got home. My sister can look like a real knockout when she makes a small effort, but now she was wearing an old frayed bathrobe and she had one of those Saturday morning plaster of paris green things on her face. Her hair was sticking up at odd angles because it had some kind of grease on it. She looked like one of those creatures in the tavern scene in *Star Wars*. "Don't you think you ought to wash your hair?" I asked.

"Don't be smart," she said, without looking up from her magazine. She took another bite of cereal and then smiled at something she was reading. Her teeth clashed with her face.

"A thing of beauty is a joy forever," I said. That made her look up from her magazine.

"You don't look so hot yourself. You've got syrup on your moustache."

Suddenly I felt insecure. But then I remembered that I would have the last laugh this morning. I had it all planned. Feeling smug all over, I dialed Al, my boss at the bindery. Al and I had an understanding. He let me come in whenever I wanted to because he knew that when I did traipse in, I worked like crazy to keep my job.

"Hi, Al," I said, watching Corker's face. "This is Ben. I just wanted you to know that I won't be in today until after lunch sometime. My good buddy . . . in fact, he's my best friend. He just got back from his mission, and I want to spend some time with him."

Corker's spoon stopped before it got to her lips, and she stared at me. Some of the Cheerios already in her mouth began to dribble down her chin because her mouth was hanging open. She quickly closed it until she remembered that her spoon was poised midway toward her mouth. She opened her mouth again and slipped the Cheerios deftly inside, forcing herself to act nonchalant.

"When did Steve get home?" she asked, after I had hung up the phone.

"Last night."

"Oh, and how is he?"

"He's a good man."

She was quiet, and she took a dainty sip of orange juice as she waited patiently for further information. I didn't give her any.

"And?" she said at last.

"And what?" We were dancing the nonchalance cha-cha.

"And how does he look?"

"Looks good. Same old Steve." When she saw the tiny smirk on my face, her eyes narrowed.

"You're not funny, Ben."

"Whatever do you mean? Could you mean you'd like to hear more? That maybe you'd like to know if he asked about you?"

"No."

She paused. "Did he?"

I felt dizzy with power, and I decided to enjoy myself by keeping her waiting once again while I downed an entire glass of orange juice at my leisure. "Yes, he asked about you," I said at last. "He said, 'How's Corker?' No, I take that back. He said, 'How's your baby sister?' "

"That sounds like a man," Corker said, trying to sound disgusted. "I could be running for Congress and Steve would say, 'How's your baby sister?' " But her mouth twitched slightly into a small half-smile, and I could tell she was pleased that Steve had asked about her.

"Don't smile, whatever you do! Your face could crack into a thousand pieces."

"Did he say anything else?" she asked.

"Yes."

"What?"

I couldn't resist it. "He said he'd be over in five minutes."

Corker jumped back from the table, knocking over her orange juice glass in the process. With her bathrobe sashes dancing behind her, she padded across the kitchen linoleum and then galloped up the stairs two, possibly three, at a time. I was pretty sure she hadn't learned to climb stairs like that in Madeline's School of Grace and Modeling. The upstairs bathroom door swung open and crashed against the wall. My face one big smirk, I went to the stairs.

"Corker," I called. "Hey, Corker!" Her face was only half green when she came to the top of the stairs. My cheeks burst into laughter.

"So help me, Ben, if you made that up. . . . Ben? Did you? Never mind, you did."

"Ah, the exquisite beauty of a woman in love! She moves with grace. She is a symphony of loveliness. Her fragile skin is as the petal of a flower. Her eyes, the moist dewdrops. Her skin . . ." I found myself mumbling through the towel she had just thrown down the stairs.

"You are definitely a creep!" she shouted.

In total satisfaction I finished her Cheerios and thumbed through her magazine. When Mom came in from the garden I was humming. "Oh, hello, Mom," I said sheepishly.

"You've been teasing again, haven't you, Ben?" I felt like a twenty-three-year-old preadolescent as I nodded.

"How did you know?"

"I can always tell by your face," she said, with a sigh in her voice.

"Somebody has to keep her humble, right?" I said.

2

It was Steve who first gave Melanie Melissa Adriana Van Vleet the name "Corker." She had been called other things in her life. With creative flair and the finesse and tact only a brother can have, I had provided her with such nicknames as "M&M" the summer her face broke out; "Smelly Melly" after she had worn too much of my mother's "Evening in Paris" perfume; and "Big Red" after her first permanent turned her hair into a large, bright bush.

For obvious reasons, those names didn't take. But neither did the other nicknames that cropped up once in a while. The people at Mom's work called her "The Ball of Fire" and "Firecracker" after she dazzled them during their lunch break with a display of fast tap dancing, poetry reciting, and intellectual prattle amazing for a ten-year-old. Even those names didn't stick. But the nickname "Corker" stuck to her like a wad of chewing gum. It was a wad of gum she wore proudly. I can still remember the first time Steve called her that.

Corker had never shown much interest in the table tennis table in our basement until the Morgans moved in next door and Steve started coming over to play a game once in a while. He was a pretty good player, and I wasn't too bad myself. Once, just for fun, Steve played Corker a game, and he wiped her out royally. I could tell that bothered Corker a great deal. But the next game when he let her win by a small margin, bothered Corker even more.

That summer, Corker started practicing. She played two, sometimes three, hours a day. When I wouldn't practice with her, she would talk Mom into playing. Corker practiced with old friends, with new friends, and once she even talked the Avon lady into a game. I became her coach, and she listened to me for a change. By the end of the summer she was good. I couldn't figure out what she was trying to pull off, and I asked her. "What are you practicing for — the Ping-Pong Olympics?"

"No," she said matter-of-factly. "I'm planning to beat Steve. But don't tell him. It's a surprise."

"Oh-ho!" I said. "Now I think I understand."

Just three weeks after her thirteenth birthday, Corker persuaded me to invite Steve over. I knew it was a setup, but I figured it would be entertaining to watch her beat her little racket to a pulp trying to win. And I knew Steve was a good sport and would get a kick out of finding out Corker was good.

"Steve!" I caught him just as he came home from his part-time job at the bakery. "Want a game of Ping-Pong?"

"Never turn one down," he answered cheerfully. "I'll go wash up and be over in five minutes." I smiled. Steve had no idea that Corker was after his scalp.

I kept the score with a low-key grin on my face as Corker played like she had never played before. My grin disappeared as Corker beat Steve three games in a row. Steve knew after the first game that we had played a trick on him. But even so he admired spunk, and when the games were over he put down his racket and shook his head. "You're a real corker, aren't you?" he said. "How did you get so good?"

Corker shrugged, and smiled at him with a sparkle of her braces. "Practiced a little," she answered. I rolled my eyeballs behind her back.

From that time on, Steve called Melanie Melissa Adriana "Corker," and she loved it. In fact, I caught her looking up the word in our dictionaries until she found the definition she liked best. I was curious and I looked it up after she was gone. She had put a book mark in our old Webster's New World Dictionary, and when I turned to the page I could understand why. It defined a corker as a remarkable person or thing.

After Steve began calling her Corker, the other Morgans soon followed his example. Gradually other friends in the neighborhood called her Corker, and then their parents. I even found myself calling her Corker. Mother was the last hold-out, but at last even she gave in.

Maybe the name stuck because it was so suitable. Corker, you see, was born a corker. I can admit that now. But don't think it was easy growing up with her. She walked early, talked early, and was getting into things from the moment she could move. "I've just got to get all that energy steered in the right direction" was my mother's theme song for her. Mom enjoyed complaining to people about Corker's early start. "The little character walked at eight months," she would say. When someone would ask how old I was when I began walking, her voice would drop considerably. "Oh, Ben. Ben was close to eighteen months. I suppose he was waiting for a ride." Then she would begin telling about Corker's antics again. She loved to tell about the time Corker had decorated the entire bathroom with Dad's shaving cream. "Why did you do it," she had asked Corker.

Corker, always ready with a quick answer, explained. "I wanted to see what it looks like in heaven." Mom had laughed through her frustration and told Dad that night.

"Well, June," he said looking at my mother impishly. "You can't complain about a child that's religious." Mom had given Dad a look of consternation. Religion was a sore spot between them, one of the few sore spots. They agreed on practically everything and loved each other deeply. But when it came to religion, Mom nagged and Dad became stubborn. He smoked, and he smoked a lot. Mom blamed herself for his death.

"I nagged too much," she said. "If I hadn't nagged him so much he would have quit on his own; I know he would have, because he was sensible. But I was always nagging him. I nagged him to his death." She never forgave herself. We moved into a different neighborhood after that, and Mom never bothered to find out which ward we were in. Pretty soon we were out of the habit of attending church.

Mom and I slowed down after Dad's death—to slow motion. I think Mom would have moved in even slower motion if she hadn't had Corker to contend with. Dad's death affected Corker oppositely. She speeded up till she became nonstop.

And at last it looked as if her energy was harnessed somewhat. Corker became top everything. When there was a book-reading contest, Corker read the most books. When there was a talent contest, she took top prize. When the elementary school took up French, Corker immersed herself in it. She became so fluent, that she was asked to teach French to the younger students. She took outside lessons in this and lessons in that, and instructors raved about her. Dancing became her specialty, and dancing instructors called her a prodigy. Mother raved about Corker. Everyone raved about my baby sister.

Adolescence should have slowed her down, but it didn't. The summer before high school, I found a list of her goals. "Well, look what I found," I said, as I started reading it aloud. " 'Learn to speak German and Spanish well, but maintain French.' Number two: 'Take as many college prep classes as possible.' Number three—"

"Give it to me," Corker said. "Give me my list." I held the paper just out of her reach.

"Hmmmm, let's see. 'Try out for as many assemblies as feasible.' And here's a good one: 'Get straight A's.' Oh, my, let's see, it gets better!"

"Give it to me," she repeated, as she tried to grab it from me again.

" 'Take lead in school play,' I laughed then. 'Win speech contest . . . Take region in debate . . . Become Dance Club President . . . Junior Class President . . . and Senior Year—President of Girls?' " I started hooting with laughter then, and Corker was really getting riled.

"Give it to me!"

"Wait, there's more . . . 'Begin dating Steve.' Did I read that right? 'Begin dating Steve?' Is that what it said? Let me read this last part again."

"It's mine!" she shrieked. "Why don't you mind your own business!"

"Oh, is this your list? Why didn't you say so." I handed it to her. "I thought it was a note to me."

"Sure you did!"

"You left it right here for me. Can't you let me keep it? I'd like to be able to get some laughs once in a while. I mean, this list is a joke, isn't it? You couldn't really think you're going to pull off all this. I mean, look at yourself. Your clothes are ugly. You don't have any style. You're . . ."

"For your information, I'm on a diet, and I'm signed up to

take some fashion and makeup classes from an expert. I'll have the look down in three months."

I hooted again.

She smiled. "You can laugh all you want to," she said, "but I'm going to do every one of the things on that list."

"Sure you are," I replied, as I peeled a banana and stuck most of it in my mouth.

"Just watch me!"

And watch her I did. By her senior year she had checked off every item on her list except the last one. Steve hadn't asked her for an official date yet; he just hung around a lot. Ten days before her graduation, Corker made an announcement to Mom and me. "I'm going to the graduation dance with Steve."

"How wonderful!" Mom said.

I was suspicious. "Does he know yet?"

"No. When he comes over tonight to play chess, he's going to ask me."

About nine that night, after Steve had left, I heard Mom ask Corker how things had worked out.

"I won," she said with satisfaction.

"The chess game?"

"That too," she answered.

I was a little disappointed that my buddy had fallen for her snare. I was even more disappointed when he continued the process. I began noticing a difference in Steve when he was around my sister. It was something in his eyes. My good friend, it seemed, had been zapped.

I think leaving Corker to go on his mission was one of the hardest things Steve had ever had to do. I suppose he knew that Corker wouldn't understand. He was right. She didn't understand at all.

After he had left, I watched Corker plunge into college with renewed gusto. So much gusto that Mom was worried about her health. She sometimes took up to twenty hours a quarter, at times even more, and she studied late into the night. When it looked as if she might run out of tuition money, she started teaching classes of her own. By demonstrating cosmetics at the same time, Corker earned more than enough to keep herself in school. But she didn't stop there. Corker managed to squeeze parties, programs, and school politics into her busy schedule.

Once again my sister was running nonstop. It was obvious she was trying to prove something to herself.

Well, Steve was home now and apparently she hadn't succeeded. I chuckled again at the thought of her racing up the stairs. After I had given her ample time to get herself pulled together and looking like a human being, I climbed the stairs to her room.

To my amusement, Corker was crouched down on her knees peeking out of the window. I wondered whether she thought her green bathrobe and flowered shower cap disguised her as one of the plants in her window well.

"See anything of interest?" I asked. I expected her to jerk at the sound of my voice, but she remained motionless as if she had known all along that I was standing in her doorway.

"He does look good, doesn't he?" she said, with a quick glance in my direction. "You're right. He really does look like the same old Steve."

"Well, go down and see him, you looney bird," I said, touched at her lack of phoniness.

"Oh, sure! Like this?"

"You could get dressed first."

"I still need to dry my hair, and my blouse is in the dryer. Besides, it would be better if I didn't see him. I really don't want to see him."

"Why not?" I asked. "Because the old heart will flutter? The old temperature will soar?"

"It already has," she confessed. Opening her closet, she pulled out a stool and sat on it. Then she faced the mirror on the inside of the door and began rummaging through a pocket of a cut-up shoe bag that hung next to the mirror. She found a fancy little box, clicked it open, and began spreading some tawny mixture on her cheeks and back toward her temples. She took off the shower cap and shook her head until she looked like the Wild Woman of Borneo. "So what?" she said then. "Half the hearts at Granite High fluttered when Steve walked by. Why should I expect to be any different. He's classy, that's why. Quietly classy, but masculine. And not for me."

That last line surprised me. "And why not?"

"You know why not." She gave me a look of disgust. "Because he's not in the plans. That's why not."

"Oh, come on!" I sat down at her desk and propped my feet up on her mini-filing cabinet. "Oh, I get it. Because he's the prince behind the big Mormon wall?" I knew Corker wasn't too keen on Mormonism.

"That's a quaint way of putting it. But I guess in a way it's true. I'd take Steve on my terms, but I don't make concessions."

"Oh, my!" I said, with the disgust I was feeling. "The hard woman. So just for once would it really hurt you to make a concession . . . for him? Go to church and be a good little Mormon. How much could that really hurt you?"

"You know I can't do things halfway." She snapped the little box shut. I knew what she meant. Corker had never been able to stick in just a big toe. She always had to take the Nestea plunge.

"So make an exception. Just for once be a half-Mormon. Who knows, maybe you'd live happily ever after."

She looked at me as if I were made of poison. "I can't do that. That wouldn't be fair to Steve or to myself. Besides, I told you, Steve just isn't in the plans anymore." Corker walked back to her window and stood behind the semisheer curtains. "I don't want to talk about it anymore," she said. "It makes me tired to think about it. I don't even think I want to see him."

"Then why are you standing by your window staring down at the Morgans' side yard?"

She smiled a gentle, small smile. "Just curious, I guess."

"Okay, it's your life." I felt like yawning again. "But just remember you can't take money or prestige with you. Families are forever."

That made Corker turn suddenly. "Get out of here. Quit preaching at me with your dumb clichés." She paused. "But you're right. Mormonism is exactly that: families. And a family just doesn't happen to be in the plans. I'm not planning to wallow my life away in a pile of dirty diapers."

"You could *wash* the diapers."

"Yes, you men have all the simple answers, don't you? It's fine for you to be a Mormon."

I felt a little guilty. One of the things I liked best about the Church was the very thing Corker didn't think she liked about it: In general, Mormon women are more home-oriented and more domestic than other women. I planned to marry an extremely young, service-oriented Mormon girl who wasn't into women's rights and whose mother had trained her to be a fantastic cook. We could swap recipes, and our life together would be one sweet feast. Of course, I would be the indisputable king of the roost. I didn't want Corker to know what I was thinking, and I decided to put her on the defensive. "Why am I your enemy when I'm just trying to be your brother?"

"Because you're a man, Ben, and it's a man's world. I just know how it is."

"You're the one who's being simplistic," I said, flipping the tie on my apron. "If it's a man's world, why do I have dishwater hands?" I realized that my statement didn't sound terribly macho. She ignored me and plopped down on her bed, checking her fingernails carefully.

"I know what I want in this world and I'm going to get it. I've been planning for years."

"You probably *will* get it if you're sure that's what you want." I had stopped laughing at her plans long ago. "Okay, dear sister." I bowed gallantly. "May you move up the ladder of success just as quickly as you climbed the stairs a little while ago."

"Go away, Ben," she said, wincing.

"I will do that. But may I tell you first what I came up to tell you? You just might want to plan your day accordingly."

"Yes, I suppose so. What?"

"I invited Steve for lunch at around one." I saw a hint of panic flash through her steel eyes, and I had to smile. My sister was a mixed-up girl.

———————— 3 ————————

The Morgans moved into the big run-down house next door to us after we'd lived on Vine for about five years. We couldn't understand why a family like that would want the place. It was a mess. But right away they started cleaning and fixing the place up. They changed the back porch into a greenhouse-type family room with big windows; added bedrooms in the basement and attic; and painted the walls throughout with clean white paint. After they'd gardened, the old place just didn't look the same. It looked pretty spiffy. I guess they had known all along that it would.

The house wasn't the only thing that changed in the neighborhood. I really don't think we were ever on their list of potentially active Mormons. I don't think they read an outline called "How to Activate Your Neighbors." But it happened. Gradually their influence began seeping over their fence and into our yard, and then into our house. Bishop Morgan, in his quiet way, fixed things for us without fanfare. Mom and Frances became close friends, and Mom soon started going to all her meetings.

It was Steve who had the greatest impact on me. I had been getting into a little trouble once in a while; the hanging-around kind of trouble. I liked to prowl around with some friends at night. Once we climbed up to the top of Highland High and painted G's on the chimney. When Edgar Allan Poe's *The Pit and the Pendulum* was playing at the Villa, we stole the dummy out from under the sharp-edged pendulum in the foyer display. We made the newspaper with that one, and we began planning bigger capers. We stole the Moffatts' truck and prowled around in it wearing gorilla costumes. We returned the truck before dawn, before the Moffatts ever knew it was gone.

Just before and right after the Morgans moved in, my friends and I had begun drinking a little just for laughs, and we smoked once in a while. We messed around with a few drugs. I told Steve about some of our adventures, but he didn't seem impressed; and I began watching him. I thought he was pretty cool for a religious guy. I liked the way he operated. He didn't seem to need the same kinds of laughs that we did, and yet he had a good sense of humor and knew how to enjoy himself. Even though he was younger, I had to admit that Steve was much more mature than I was.

It didn't take much to get me to the ward that first night. Steve just mentioned a party with "make-your-own" banana splits, and I was ready fast. The cute girls I saw there kept me coming.

By introducing me to a new group of friends, Steve helped me begin making a transition back to Mormonism. I quit prowling at night, and I began changing. I got plenty of laughs and attention at the ward affairs, and pretty soon I didn't need the other stuff. I cleaned up my language because it wasn't acceptable anymore, and I started cleaning up my life. When in Rome, do as the Romans do. Steve stuck by me and became a buddy I could talk to about anything. Even after he and Corker had a thing going, he never quit being my friend too.

And now he was home from his mission and coming to lunch. The world looked good, and I whistled as I stirred the white sauce for the clam chowder I was making.

I wasn't surprised when Corker showed up in the kitchen. "Decided to join us for lunch, huh?"

"I might as well get this over with," she answered brusquely. "I've got to face the music sometime."

For someone who just wanted to "get this over with," she had spent a great deal of time on her appearance. Corker looked polished, pressed and color-coordinated from the top of her auburn-gold head to the tips of her brownish-red toenails. It still amazed me that my sister could look like high-fashion with a gob of this and a dab of that.

"Well, at least you look better than you did this morning," I said. I was observing the unwritten rule that a brother should never compliment his sister unless that compliment has been reduced to its lowest recognizable form.

"Thanks loads," she mumbled, as she picked up a carrot stick and took a careful bite. "I don't imagine you want my help."

"You mean like you helped me make the sc—"

"Don't say it! You've been reminding me about those giant scones for years now. Remember the scones! Remember the Alamo!"

She was right. It was getting old; and, in truth, I did need some help. The morning had disappeared too quickly. I had begun watching TV and had fallen asleep in front of it. Mom was still busy with the laundry, and it was getting close to one o'clock.

"Do you think you could handle the carrots? I need some more peeled and cut."

Corker looked surprised that I was willing to let her help. "Oh, okay," she said uncertainly.

I began whistling again as I added a little more milk to the white sauce. When I glanced over to see how Corker was doing, I stopped whistling. "What on earth . . . I wanted carrot sticks, not carrot stubbies."

"I thought these were for the chowder. Make yourself clear, Ben."

"The vegetables for the clam chowder are already cooking. It looks like you can't handle the carrots," I said, grabbing the peeler away from her. "Why don't you make a Jell-O salad. Nobody can ruin Jell-O, not even you. You *do* know how to make Jell-O, don't you?"

"Not really," she replied.

"That figures. Well, just follow the simple instructions on the package." I opened the cupboard to show her where we kept the Jell-O.

"Lemon okay?" she asked. I was surprised she was still with me.

"Lemon's fine."

"Okay. I guess I need a bowl, don't I?"

"Good thinking! Get a pan and boil some water. That means you wait until little bubbles form."

"No kidding!" She jerked back in mock surprise as she laid the unopened package of Jell-O in the bowl.

"You were planning on opening that, weren't you?"

"Maybe I'd better open this package instantly!" She began ripping at the cardboard as she glared at me. Suddenly she backed away with a sincere look of horror on her face. "Now look what you made me do. I tore my thumbnail. Oh, that makes me mad! Here, you put on this water. I've got to go."

I shook my head and mumbled something into the white sauce.

When Corker finally came back into the kitchen, I caught her smiling at herself in the mirror over the sink, first with her teeth showing and then with her lips together.

"I'd say the first smile," I volunteered. "You might as well show your teeth, since it looks like you polished them individually." Corker stopped smiling immediately but ignored my comment as she turned from the mirror and looked up at the kitchen clock.

"What time did you say he was coming?" she asked, smoothing her hands over her slacks.

"One."

She looked at her watch and then back at the clock again. "One?"

"One."

"It's after one now."

"Yes, it looks like it's a minute and a half after one. That means he'll be strolling along shortly." I suspected his "strolling along shortly" was precisely what was worrying her. "Do you remember that Jell-O water that we decided should be boiled for the Jell-O?"

"Yes."

"It's boiling."

She glanced at the back burner and saw that I was speaking the truth.

"How about making some Jell-O?" I suggested. "The quick-set method. The instructions are on the package."

"Okay," she said, with hesitancy. I think Corker would have been able to handle her small assignment if at that moment the

Morgans' screen door hadn't slammed. Footsteps, presumably Steve's, were crunching down the driveway as Corker carried the pan of boiling water to the bowl on the counter. She stared at the back door screen, and I stared at her as she poured the water over the half-opened package of lemon Jell-O.

"I thought you planned to open that Jell-O first," I said, trying to remain calm. "And I also assumed you would measure the water. That looks more like five or six cups than two cups."

"Oh." She stared blankly into the bowl of steaming water, and I was concerned that in her present mental state she might reach into the water and try to retrieve the package.

"Hot! Water—hot! No, no!" I reminded her. "Here." I grabbed the tongs out of the utensil drawer. But Corker had seen the top of Steve's head as he climbed our porch, and she pulled one of the quickest disappearance routines I have ever seen.

"Can't handle it, huh?" I shouted after her. "Yes, go read some more affirmation cards!"

Steve looked puzzled as he tapped on our screen. "Come in," I said. "Sit down. Take your shoes off. Boy, am I glad to see you! Corker is a little nervous, and she's driving me crazy."

"I'm a little nervous myself," he said gently. Steve didn't look nervous, just freshly showered, shaved, and immaculately groomed. His light hair was still a little damp.

"You? What for?" He shrugged without peeling his eyes off the hall.

"She should be right back," I promised. "Sit down." Steve sat down obediently, stretched his hands, and looked toward the counter. After a few seconds he began tapping the table with his fingers. Now *I* was getting nervous.

We've got to get this over with, I thought. "Corker!" I called. "Steve's here, and he wouldn't mind saying hello to you." That made Steve sit up a little and clear his throat. But Corker didn't appear.

"Hey, just relax," I said. "Be cool. It's just Corker. You remember Corker, the kid with the freckles and the red pigtails."

"Your little sister is a big girl now," Steve said. It sounded like a song from a "Sesame Street" I had watched with Joshua once. Steve looked as if he planned to tap the table again.

"Corker!" I shouted.

"I think she wants to be announced formally," I said to Steve. I was beginning to get worried that Corker had slipped out the front. When she still didn't show, Steve stood up and walked to the counter to pick up a carrot stick. I saw him looking at the bowl of Jell-O water with curiosity on his face. Before I had a chance to explain, Corker appeared in the doorway. At the precise moment that Corker said "Hello, Steve" with just the right inflection and toughness in her voice, Steve was yanking his hand out of the water and shaking his fingers. "Hot!" he said.

"You didn't just do that, did you?" I asked.

"No, I didn't," he answered. "At least, I wish I hadn't."

When she realized what had happened, Corker suddenly forgot she was the woman of steel and turned into Florence Nightingale. She rushed to the sink and turned on the cold water. Next she grabbed Steve's hand and pulled him along with it to the cold stream. "I read once that cold water is best for burns," she said excitedly. "Hurry!"

The water had been pouring over their fingers for a few seconds when their eyes met for the first time.

"Hello, there." Steve's face registered amusement, and Corker's lips twisted into a small smile.

"Hello," she said, rather softly for an assertive woman. "Are you okay?" Then she seemed to remember who she was and what she stood for, and she stepped back slightly. "I'm sorry about your hand," she said, rather formally. "It was my fault. I'm the one who left the package in the bowl."

"She thought it was the quick-set method," I added.

"It doesn't hurt that badly," Steve said, still looking at her. His light eyes twinkled. "It just smarted for a second or two."

"You're probably just saying that." Corker's hazel eyes looked lighter than usual.

"No, really, it doesn't hurt that much now."

"That's a relief," Corker said, releasing his hand quickly.

"On second thought, it might still smart a little." He took back her hand. "By the way . . ." he paused. "It's good to see you, Corker." He nodded. "It's really good to see you," he repeated slowly, looking into her eyes at close range.

She seemed hypnotized for a few seconds as she returned his stare. Then she stretched her eyes a little and bit her bottom lip slightly. "Yes . . . yes . . . well . . . well . . ." She laughed nervously and turned toward the counter to escape his gaze. When she picked up the relish tray, I noticed that it was shaking and so were Corker's lips, but she tried to fake it. "And it's good to see you too, Steve," she said in a businesslike, woman-of-steel manner. "We've all missed you—Ben, Mom, and I . . ." But her voice gave her away, and Steve was smiling gently as he watched her.

I turned quickly because I didn't want them to see me grinning widely. I removed the clam chowder from the back burner and decided to forget about the salad. Steve and Corker wouldn't notice what they were eating anyway, I determined. "Mom," I shouted. "Mom, if you are within the sound of my voice, please come at once. The chowder is cooling fast!" *And that's the only thing that's cooling around here,* I thought to myself.

For former debate champions, Corker and Steve did not have a great deal to say during lunch. Mom and I felt the pressure and carried the entire conversational burden on our shoulders. I started off the luncheon with a bang by giving Corker full credit for the carrot sticks. Mom seemed to know immediately which ones Corker had cut. "How interesting! Little chips rather than sticks." Corker smiled mysteriously.

"They're very nice." Steve picked up one of the small discs. "Clever." He took a careful bite to avoid crunching on his finger. "Good, too," he added quickly.

"I'm glad you like them," Corker said, pleased that her carrot stubbies had been such a success. She looked at me with raised eyebrows.

While Mom and I talked effusively, Corker and Steve limited their conversation to one- and two-word sentences. I finished off my joke repertoire and the silence fell thick. Only the sound of sipping chowder could be heard until my mother cleared her throat. "Well," she said. Her butter knife was poised in the air, and I knew she planned to slice the silence. "Tell us about your mission, Steve."

"I'll have to do that sometime," Steve said. He took a bite of chowder and watched Corker take a bite of hers. Mother looked at me helplessly and tried again.

"Well, why not now? You know what they say about there being no time like the present."

Steve smiled. "They do say that, don't they? But it would take too long."

"Oh, yes, I guess it would." My mother relented. "I guess it would be just like you asking us to tell you about the last two years of our lives. Where would we begin?" She paused and looked at me. "Well, I guess we would begin with my transfer at the telephone company. And then Corker. . . ."

Mother began giving Steve a two-year rundown. He seemed interested, and that encouraged Mother to go into detail with enthusiasm and inflection. Mom did quite a comprehensive job, although she did neglect to mention my second trip to the dentist and my root canal. I could tell she was bushed by the time she had finished. I was tired too.

By now it was pretty obvious that Steve and Corker needed to be alone. "I'll bet Steve didn't listen to music on his mission, Corker," I said. "Maybe he'd like to listen to some albums. I think Mom and I can handle the dishes." Corker apparently didn't feel at all confident yet about being alone with Steve, because she began shaking her head slightly and she peered at me with panic in her expression. I pretended not to get the message. She stared at me again to get my attention. When Steve looked at her, however, she smiled quickly.

"Steve just got home," she said. "I'm sure he still needs to unpack, and I'm sure he has plenty to do. I don't suppose you'd want to listen to music right now, would you, when you have so much to do?"

"I wouldn't mind listening to some good music," Steve answered.

"Oh, you mean later, don't you?"

"Yes, or right now."

"Right now, huh?" Corker stood up. "Well, why don't we help in the kitchen first?"

"We can handle things in here," I said. "You two go ahead." *Remember, Sis,* I thought, *you've got to face the music sometime.*

Corker frowned at me and I grinned back. It amused and amazed me that my sister—the superwoman, the woman of steel—was afraid. I suspected she wasn't afraid of Steve, but of herself.

The minute they closed the door to the living room, Mom clapped her hands together softly and then held them to her mouth. "Oh, Ben, I'm so thrilled. It was so wonderful of you to get them together for lunch. I think they're still in love."

"Why do you think that?" I asked.

25

"Isn't it obvious?" My mother began energetically stacking the bowls and then the bread plates.

"You mean because they were acting like looney birds?"

"Exactly."

I began laughing as I remembered Corker's face. "She was scared," I said. "Scared silly. Can you imagine Corker scared?"

"Shhhh," Mom said. "They'll hear you." She ran the hot water into the right-hand sink and put in a few shots of dishwater detergent. While she giggled, I chuckled. After she had run the rinse water into the left sink, she grew quiet. "Shhhh," she said again when I tried to warn her that her sleeve was hanging in the water. "Let's listen." Mom bit her bottom lip and grinned when bursts of laughter and vigorous talking could be heard from the living room. "They're talking!" she said. "Isn't it exciting!" She scrubbed a pan with renewed energy, placed it carefully on the drawing board, dried her hands on the kitchen towel, and removed her apron.

"I've got to call Frances and tell her," she said. She listened again carefully for a moment, grinned, and hurried into the bedroom.

I shook my head as she bounced from the kitchen, but I smiled as I clicked on the small TV on the counter and pulled up two kitchen chairs, one for my feet. My eyes wandered from the bowling game on the tube to the refrigerator and then back to the bowling game. *It wouldn't hurt me to skip dessert for once,* I told myself, trying to sound convincing. Steve hadn't gained an ounce on his mission and was still tight and slim. I had turned into a year-round Santa Claus. But I kept staring at the fridge and at the little turkey magnet with the sign that someone had given us for Thanksgiving that read, "You are what you eat."

"I don't care right now," I said quietly. "Because, let's face it, I'm still hungry. I'll start my diet tomorrow, for sure." Five minutes later I was taking a huge bite of strawberry shortcake with a double layer of whipping cream.

I had licked my lips and taken another bite before I noticed that the living room was rather quiet. *Hmmmm,* I said to myself, as I waited for the lively talking to return. When no sounds emerged, a Cheshire cat grin spread on my face. *Way to go, Steve,* I thought.

With a giant bite of cake in my mouth, I walked into the hall and checked to see what my mother was doing. It looked as if she would be busy for a while writing in her journal, and I walked to the counter and picked up a dishcloth. While I wiped the table, I began working my way around it toward the wall. Again I listened. All was quiet. Inching my way against the wall, I headed for the tiny crack of an opening in the door. Two years before, I would have made it past the chair that blocked my path, but now I was stuck and I had to move the chair with a squeak. I froze before I continued. When nothing happened, I again began sliding against the wall. At last I could see Corker and Steve sitting on the couch in the living room facing each other.

I have always had twenty-twenty vision, but what I saw made me squint. My sister's cheeks were pulled in, forming a little fishy mouth. Her eyes were crossed and her thumbs were in her ears. As far as I could tell, Steve's reaction was deadpan. His mouth only twitched slightly.

"You're good," Corker said. "You didn't even come close to laughing."

It struck me as amazing that my sister, who had spent at least two hours getting ready, would now be pulling fishy faces.

"Okay, are you ready?" Steve asked. He stood up in a dignified manner and turned his back to her. Suddenly he jumped around with the face of an ape. Corker stared at him as he scratched and jumped up and down. Her eyes grew wide, but she retained her smileless state. Soon, however, her cheeks began to puff out and her face pinkened, but she didn't laugh.

"Are you sure you're not laughing?" Steve said.

She shook her head.

"Uh-huh, *now* you are."

She shook her head again.

"Okay, you're not laughing."

Corker spurted out the air in her cheeks.

"Now tell me you weren't laughing."

"Okay, I guess I was laughing. It's my turn again," she said eagerly. "This time I'm going to get you."

I backed away from the door slowly and sat down at the kitchen table. I leaned my chin in my hands and stared at the door, scratching my temples. I was still staring at the door when Mother came back into the kitchen. When she noticed the quiet in the living room, she winked at me mischievously. I didn't wink back.

"Mom," I whispered, as I motioned her to come closer. "Would it strike you as unusual that two attractive, intelligent, achievement-oriented, mature people with high IQ's who are crazy about each other and haven't seen each other for two years, would be pulling faces at each other?"

Mother looked at me doubtfully. "What do you mean, pulling faces?" she asked.

"Pulling faces," I said. "Like this." I pulled a fishy face, crossed my eyes, and stuck my thumbs in my ears.

"Oh, you mean pulling faces. No, not in the least." She tried to sound convincing, but she lowered her eyebrows and tiptoed straightforwardly to the crack in the door. She took a quick peek through the crack, smiled at me sideways, and tiptoed back to the table. "I should have known you were just pulling my leg, you character," she whispered, with satisfaction in her voice.

"Oh?" I raised my eyebrows.

She nodded and tried to hide a little smirk which was fighting to emerge. "They just needed to be alone," she whispered. "Let's celebrate. Where's that cake. I don't think they'll need dessert, do you?" she asked with the same mischievous look.

After she had joined me with a piece of strawberry shortcake, she began talking affably. "I saw the most elegant cake at a country club once. It was an exclusive club and the cake was . . . well, it was just gorgeous. It won't sound like it when I explain it, but it was gorgeous. I just know you and I could make it. It had four layers; and this sounds strange, but there were fresh flowers on one side. It was just gorgeous."

"What are you talking about," I asked.

"A wedding cake I saw once," my mother said happily.

"A wedding cake?"

"Yes. The kind of fresh flowers we used would depend on the colors Corker decides on. I mean, that girl definitely has her own mind, but I just know she'd go along with the cake. That same wedding had these beautiful little bowls on each table, with lavender water and tiny flowers floating in them. And they served lots of fresh fruits." I was happy to see that Mother had high hopes for Corker and Steve, but I thought planning their wedding was going a little far.

"Mom," I said.

"You're right, she should decide on the refreshments. I'll leave it up to her."

"Mom," I repeated. "Are you planning to pick names for your grandchildren next?"

"Oh, no. They'd have to pick their own names for their children. Oh, but they'll have some lovely children! I hope they pick lovely names. They're so perfect for each other, aren't they, Ben?" she said, patting my hand with her plump smaller hand.

I thought of them pulling faces at each other. "Yes, aren't they." I paused. "But, Mom, I think you might be underestimating Corker's ambition. She still wants to—"

"Let me level with you," my mother continued. "You're probably concerned about where I would get the money for an extravagant reception, aren't you? Well, you don't need to worry about a thing, Ben. I've been saving for this wedding since the Morgans moved in."

"No kidding!" I said in awe. "You've been saving up since you first met Steve?"

"Of course," she said. "A mother can just tell some things." She took another happy bite of whipping cream. "It had kind of a cream frosting."

"What?"

"The cake I saw," she said.

4

Summer is a good time for sunburns, vacations, sleeping in lawn chairs, homemade ice cream, and love. Corker and Steve were in love, and everyone knew it. They hadn't mentioned it to anyone. They didn't need to. Steve had been home three weeks, and I was beginning to wonder if face-pulling held some magical power of attraction that I wasn't aware of. I figured that every day Corker stayed home was a plus point for Steve and a minus point for New York.

It was Saturday, and I was sitting on the porch waiting for them to return from the Homestead because I wanted to catch them before I left for the bindery. I had planned carefully what I would say, but I wouldn't say it carefully. I'd say it casually, as if it really didn't matter—more as if it were a flash through my mind.

At last Steve's blue Pontiac turned the corner and stopped in front. Steve helped Corker out of the car and they laughed and swung the picnic basket between them. Joshua and Billy Patrick tumbled out of the back and ran up to me. I flipped them each a nickel and suggested they run home and let their moms know they were back. Then I cleared my throat and stretched a little.

Corker looked sunburned and a bit freckled, and her hair seemed less organized, but Steve didn't seem to mind. Ah, love! He had to peel his eyes away from her to acknowledge me.

"Hey, you should have come with us," he said. "We really had a good time, didn't we?"

"It was a super day," Corker said, looking as if she really meant it.

Steve laughed. "We taught Joshua and Billy to dive by throwing pennies in the water. You should have seen them go."

"Steve's good with kids," Corker said. "And he's an excellent diver."

"Really, next time come with us," Steve said again.

I realized that I was almost passing by a good opening for the idea I wanted to present. "I should have," I said. "I just lazed around this afternoon, as usual. But—" I paused. "Well, maybe we could double-date sometime. I was thinking maybe this weekend. Next Saturday sound okay?"

"Sounds great," Steve said. "Anybody we know?"

Now, just when my voice needed to sound casual, I could feel a golf ball of some kind getting stuck in my throat. "Well, I thought maybe your leggy baby sister would like to come along."

"Darlene?" Steve looked surprised.

"Sure, why not? I could do worse."

"I don't know. She might already be busy next Saturday. She's pretty involved—dates a lot, and—"

"Well, there's no harm in your asking." I was beginning to mumble.

"My asking? Wait a minute. Why don't *you* ask her?" Suddenly Steve smiled and decided to rib me a little. "Nervous?"

"Nervous? Why?" We could both hear the golf ball now. "A little," I admitted.

"Hey, just relax. Be cool," he said grinning. "It's only Darlene. You remember Darlene—brown pigtails, braces."

"Little sister is a big girl now?" I asked sheepishly.

"Just barely," Corker said.

Steve folded his arms and stared at me for a moment. "Well, okay, I'll ask her, since you're a buddy. What did you have in mind?"

"Let's go see *Superman II*—the comeback. I can spare a buck or two."

Corker rolled her eyeballs. "Last of the big spenders," she said.

"Do you want to ask Darlene *now* before you forget?" I asked Steve.

"Right now?" He looked at Corker. "I don't think she's home right now."

"She's home," I said too quickly. "I saw her biking in just a half-hour ago."

"Okay, but don't get your hopes up. Want to come along, Corker."

"No," Corker said, "but I'll wait for you."

"Okay." He kept looking at her.

"Are you sure you two can stand being apart for three whole minutes?" I asked. "She said she'd wait for you. What more can you ask?"

Steve smiled and touched Corker's nose with his forefinger. "You really got sunburned," he said. "Let me kiss it better." A quick peck on her nose, and he was gone.

"Oh, brother!" I said.

"Oh, brother, to you!" Corker said.

"Oh, brother, what?" I asked defensively.

"Darlene *is* a little young for you, you know."

"She's legal age — eighteen."

"Just barely eighteen."

"Lots of men date younger women. It's the best time to train them," I said. *And*, I thought, *what eighteen-year-old wouldn't give her eye-teeth to go out with an older man?*

"Oh, really!" Corker puckered her mouth in disgust and looked sideways with what my mother always called her Jack Benny look. She picked up the picnic basket then, and with a glance in the direction of Steve's house, and a soft smile, she went into the house.

I was glad she was gone so that I could wait nervously in private. I assumed Steve would come back right away and tell me what Darlene had said. But he didn't come back right away. I wandered into the house, picked up the latest copy of the *Reader's Digest*, flipped through it quickly to "Life in These United States," and then wandered back out again and into the backyard. I sat in the lawn chair behind the rose bush, the closest chair to the Morgans' kitchen window. But I couldn't hear much — just muffled voices, and the radio playing rather loudly.

Apparently Joshua had seen me go into the backyard, because a moment or two later he was sitting by my feet rubbing a dandelion and getting yellow all over his palm. He seemed more quiet than usual. I patted his head. "How's it going, Tiger?"

Joshua remained quiet. Finally he spoke. "Big Ben?"

"Yeah?"

"What's a pound winkling?"

I hadn't been paying much attention to Joshua, because my eyes were glued to the Morgans' back door.

"A pound winkling?" I said, humoring him. "Hmmmmm, a pound winkling? I give up. What's a pound winkling?"

Normally when I didn't know the answer to his riddle he would jump up and begin laughing. But now he remained quiet and he didn't come up with the punchline. "What's a pound winkling?" I repeated.

He shrugged. "I don't know."

I looked down at him then. "What do you mean, you don't know? Did you forget the answer to your riddle?"

"It's not a riddle," he said.

"What is it, then?"

"I don't know. Darlene said you was a pound winkling."

"Darlene said I was a pound winkling." Suddenly Joshua had my undivided attention. "When did Darlene say I was a pound winkling?" I asked, trying not to frighten Joshua with too much eagerness. "Did Darlene say that just now? Were you, by any chance, just in your house?"

He nodded.

"Joshua," I said slowly. "Did Darlene say that when Steve asked her if she wanted to go on a date with me?"

Joshua nodded again.

"And what else did she say?"

He shrugged. "I can't remember."

"Let's pretend something," I said. "I'll be Steve and you be Darlene."

Joshua wrinkled his nose. "I don't want to be a girl."

"Just for this once, humor me. Okay, I'm Steve, and I say, 'Hey, Darlene, do you want to go to the show Saturday with Corker and me and Big Ben?' "

"No way," Joshua said.

"No way? What do you mean, 'no way'? Did Darlene say 'no way' or are you saying 'no way' because you don't want to be a girl?"

"Darlene said 'No way. Because Ben is a pound winkling.' "

"Oh!" I winced as I wondered what a pound winkling was. I had the feeling it wasn't good. "Because Ben is a pound winkling?"

"Yes, a three-hundred one."

Suddenly the pieces began fitting together. *Because Ben is a three-hundred-pound winkling . . . weakling.* " 'No way, because Ben is a three-hundred pound weakling.' Is that what Darlene said?"

Joshua nodded.

"I see," I said. The golf ball had slipped to the pit of my stomach, but mostly I was angry. "I see," I said again. "Because Ben is a three-hundred-pound weakling," I repeated. "The little twirp. I don't weigh anywhere near three-hundred pounds. And a weakling, huh? Oh, really, a weakling!"

"Big Ben," Joshua said, "I'll go to the show with you."

"Thanks anyway, little buddy," I answered. "But I think I can get another date."

I hadn't weighed myself for quite a while, but I went right into the house and into the bathroom to stand on the scale. I knew I wouldn't be anywhere near three hundred pounds. I was right. I only weighed 267 pounds. I was a whole thirty-three pounds away from three hundred pounds. *Thirty-three pounds is a lot of weight to be away from three-hundred pounds,* I thought. *How would Darlene like me to accuse her of being thirty-three pounds more than she weighs,* I wondered. *And a weakling. Me, a weakling? A puny girl like Darlene calls me a weakling.* Darlene couldn't have weighed more than 120 pounds. She was five feet six at the most. I was six feet three and a half and she was calling *me* a weakling. She was skin and bones — true they were very nice bones, but just the same she was skin and bones, with just a few soft curves — mostly bones, and she was calling *me* a weakling. "Three hundred pound weakling," I muttered again. I was getting angrier and angrier.

What motivates a human being to act? What motivates a human being to quit putting off something that needs to be done? I would like to be able to say that I became motivated to do something about my weight and physical health because my body is a temple and I wanted to improve that temple of my spirit. Or, because I wanted to live the Word of Wisdom with more fullness. Yes, I would like to be able to say that, but that was not my reason. My reason was much less noble. I began a diet and exercise program because Darlene Morgan called me a three-hundred-pound weakling.

My alarm woke me up the next morning, but it was not my alarm that got me out of bed. It was the words "three-hundred-pound weakling" that got me out of bed. I suddenly remembered again, and I pushed myself out of the sack with a roll. I had made myself a goal sheet, the kind that Corker always makes. My methods for achieving my goals listed weight-lifting, swimming, tennis, basketball, jumping rope, bicycling, and of course jogging. In two months I planned to look somewhat like a thinner version of the poster of Rocky that I had found in a drawer and hung up in my room.

The first month I planned to lose a great deal of weight. Then I'd gain weight back the second month, but this time it would be hard muscle—hard biceps; thick chest with indented stomach; firm, big legs, devoid of flab; broad shoulders; bison neck. When Darlene swooned over the new me, I'd say, "Eat your heart out, Darlene, I'm not interested in twirps."

I slipped into my T-shirt and my somewhat snug jogging pants and I tried on the running shoes I had bought on a good sale two years before. Then I peeked out of the back door. If I hurried, I could make it back before Darlene was even up. I planned to take it slowly at the start. This morning I would only run two miles or so. I could work up to three by the end of the week. Taking a deep breath, I beat my chest like King Kong. *Look out, world!* I thought. *It's me, Big Ben, and I'm out to get in shape.* I frowned as I passed the Morgans' and winced again. *Just wait, Darlene!* I thought.

I had barely passed the Morgans' and rounded their corner when I knew I probably wouldn't make it quite the full two miles. *I'm just a little out of breath,* I thought, as I snorted like a campground skunk looking for a bite to eat. I tried to keep my mouth shut, but my chest seemed to be rattling and I needed more air. My stomach and buttocks felt unattached to the rest of me, as if I were a running water-bed. By the time I had passed the tennis courts I was wheezing and panting.

But I was encouraged. The tightening process had already begun in my legs. They were firming up already; I could feel it.

And my chest was already thickening with muscle. I could feel the thickness. I could also feel a gnawing ache in my right side, however, which concerned me. I wondered whether an appendectomy hurt a great deal. I pictured myself being carried off on a stretcher, and the thought was gratifying. Soon my left side also hurt, and I ruled out appendicitis.

By now I was determined to make it at least one mile. But my mouth was parched, and phlegm was developing in my throat. My lungs must have been filled with mothballs, because I could feel them stuffed inside my chest cavity. I wondered why they made jogging shoes so heavy. My legs could hardly lift them. With one last effort I ran two more houses to the school ground lawn. Heaving huge sighs of air, I tried to lift my feet, but I could no longer pick them up. My jogging shoes had turned to lead. My T-shirt was sopping, and the perspiration was rolling like a river of salt water down my face and neck. My heart, I was afraid, would burst — and I hadn't bothered to get a physical checkup before running. I *had* to stop. Gulping for air, I collapsed on the lawn. I had run *two blocks.*

After I had coughed for a while and rested for another while, some moisture began returning to my mouth and my breathing was almost normalized, with only an occasional giant heave. Rolling to a crawling position, I stood up with a grunt, but I couldn't stand upright and I stooped like an old man. I plodded home with a slight limp, my hand holding the ache that persisted in my left side.

After I had passed the tennis courts, I noticed with horror Steve and Darlene talking near the picket fence that I would need to pass. I looked at my wet T-shirt and my huge tight canary-yellow pants, and I thought of my face looking flushed and uncool. Quickly I ducked behind the pigeon coop that Billy Patrick had gotten special permission to build in the field right behind the Morgans' yard. I hoped my bright yellow could not be spotted through the cracks.

Sitting in squat position was painful and tedious, but I didn't dare move for fear someone would hear me and find me hunched over looking like a fool. I sat there, *feeling* like a fool for several minutes, until I decided to walk on my haunches to the edge of the pigeon coop and peek around. It had grown quiet at the Morgans'. When I saw that Darlene and Steve had disappeared back into the house, I began the tedious process of raising my aching body.

Using the coop as a support, I began lifting myself, but a sudden pain shot through me and I lowered myself again. I decided I needed to stretch my leg before I rose, because I couldn't seem to get myself into proper position. I was trying again, when I felt a splat on the back of my neck and down my T-shirt. I didn't need to check and see what had hit me. Above me a gray pigeon with dark markings was cooing contentedly. She began grooming the feathers on her neck, ignoring me totally. *So far this hasn't been my day,* I thought. I pulled my shoulders back as another pain ripped down my side.

"Crooooo, Croooooo," the pigeon said.

I looked up at her with malice. "Oh, yeah! Well, may your tail feathers be plucked out one by one by a condor chasing you through twisting canyons," I said. "May you be hung by your beak in front of a hummingbird feeder . . . May you . . ." I decided to move quickly.

The front of the Morgans' corner home can't be seen until you round the corner and pass the forsythia bush. To my dismay, I saw that maybe Steve had gone into the house, but Darlene hadn't. She had relocated to the front porch and was tying her shoes. Luckily, the Morgans have a large front yard, and I knew she wouldn't get the close-up she would have had before; but I was sure that even from far away I didn't look good. Pulling my body straighter, I suddenly lost the limp and I began running again with a forced bounce in my step that almost killed me.

"Big Ben!" Darlene called out, with surprise in her voice. "I didn't know you ran. How did you do?"

I held up two fingers as I sprinted painfully toward my driveway.

"Two miles is absolutely super for a beginner!" Darlene called, and I could hear the admiration in her voice.

I was panting heavily and couldn't have answered her verbally if I had wanted to, as I jaunted up the porch steps. I turned around, smiled and waved, shut the door, and collapsed on the kitchen floor.

Perhaps it was Darlene whose well-chosen words motivated me to begin planning my exercise campaign and thereby started me out on my first jogging adventure. But in all fairness, Corker should be credited with giving me the motivation to continue.

After a shower, I limped into the kitchen and opened the fridge. Corker was sitting at the kitchen table, flipping through three-by-five cards like a card shark. She watched me take out the cheesecake and looked back down when I looked at her. At this moment I was not fond of my baby sister, who could fulfill personal goals faster than I could make them. I suspected that she could get up, run three circles around me, and be seated again before I could even find a chair. It annoyed me that she had been sitting there flipping through her success cards, while I was outside suffering and sitting under birds. "Have a piece of cheesecake," I said angrily.

"No, thanks."

"No, thanks," I mimicked. "Just for once, why don't you say, 'Yes, Ben, I'd love one. I'd love to share a piece of cheesecake with you.' "

"Okay," she replied, looking up. "Yes, Ben, I'd love to share a piece of cheesecake with you. I really would."

"Good," I said, lifting my knife to cut her a piece and hoping she'd instantly gain three pounds.

"But I've already had breakfast."

"That figures. You know what you are? You are a robot-woman in high gear. Just for once why don't you try being a human being with flesh and blood, a real person with weak-nesses instead of a self-disciplined piece of steel?"

"If I were a self-disciplined piece of steel without weak-nesses," she answered quietly, "I wouldn't still be in Salt Lake right now, would I." She paused and turned her head at an angle as she looked at me. "By the way, how was jogging this morning?"

"How did you know I went jogging?"

"I noticed you were wearing jogging shoes as you crawled toward the shower about half an hour ago. How far did you get?"

"Not far."

"How far?"

"Get off my back."

"How far?"

"Two lousy blocks," I said, plopping down in a chair, my cheesecake in front of me.

"Two blocks?" I expected her to begin laughing. "Two blocks—really?"

"Yes, two blocks. That's what I said."

"Two blocks is fantastic!"

"Oh, sure!"

"No, really. I didn't think you'd get further than the tennis courts."

"Thanks a lot," I said. "Two blocks is bad enough."

She was quiet then. "Two blocks is a whole lot better than nothing, isn't it?" she said at last.

She had a point, and I didn't put the cheesecake in my mouth right away. I just kept cutting at it with my fork. I grunted, and that gave her encouragement to scamper up onto her soapbox and begin lecturing. "A person can do anything . . . anything he wants to in this life if he's willing to work at it. But he has to be willing to admit he's on the bottom rung or wherever he's at in order to begin," she said with conviction. "And that may just be the hardest part."

"Yes, well, I'm at the bottom rung, all right. I planned to be in shape in a few weeks or a month or two. At the rate I'm going I would barely be getting into shape by my birthday, and on my birthday I'll be twenty-four—an old man." I could even *feel* the misery in my voice.

"So how old will you be if you don't get into shape?" Corker asked.

Twenty-four, I thought, but I just grunted again. I didn't want Corker to know I thought she had made another good point.

"Wouldn't you rather be a strong, slim, tight twenty-four-year-old than an out-of-shape twenty-four-year-old?"

Yes, I thought, feeling glad she hadn't used the word *fat.* I kept cutting my cheesecake into smaller and smaller pieces, and then I stared at them. I could almost taste them melting on my tongue. *It would be a shame to waste this cheesecake,* I thought. *But on the other hand, it would turn to fat if I ate it, and that would be a waste. I wonder if Foxtrot likes cheesecake.* Without further comment, I picked up the plate, put it back in the fridge, and traded it for two oranges.

5

"I'm a winner! I'm a winner!" I repeated, as I forced my aching legs to rise and fall. "I can make it! Just a few more steps! 189 ... 190 ... 191 ..."

Today I planned to run on my mini-tramp to my approximate weight, 260 pounds—a step for each pound. My exact weight now was 257 pounds. Before, when I had weighed myself, I hadn't considered my clothing, which must have weighed about seven pounds, making me 260 pounds not 267 pounds. Now I had lost three pounds, and the nice part about it was, I was still filling up. I had made a switcheroo, however. Now I was concentrating on a lot of fresh fruits, vegetables, and protein instead of bakery products. I drank five to six glasses of water a day. Just this morning I had eaten half a cantaloupe, two eggs, and a bowl of raisin bran. I finished off the meal with two glasses of orange juice. A growling stomach has never been my style.

"230 ... 231 ... 232 ..." I was gasping now, but that wasn't too bad. When I had first started, I found myself gasping before I reached one hundred.

"Are you sure that thing's strong enough to hold you?" Corker asked, as she leaned in the TV room doorway, her arms folded.

I held up my hand to indicate that I was counting and couldn't be interrupted. "243 ... 244 ... I'm a winner! I can do it! I can do it! ... 250 ... 251 ... Winner! Winner!"

"What are you shooting for?"

"259 . . . 260!" I threw my fist into the air, but I kept jogging. "Hold on, I think I can make it to three hundred . . . 270 . . . 71 . . . 72 . . . 295 . . . 299 . . . 300!" This time both my fists shot into the air to indicate victory. I had surpassed my expectations. *I'm a three-hundred-steps-winner!* I thought.

"Why don't you run outside, like other people?" Corker asked.

"Too many pigeons," I mumbled, as I clicked on the TV and plopped into the bean-bag chair.

"Too many pigeons?"

"Uh-huh." That, of course, was not my real reason. My real reason was that I was not about to risk again having anyone see me plodding out there, especially not Darlene. The next time I went outside, I planned to look like a winner. I'd wait until Darlene had begun jogging, and then I would shoot ahead of her like a human cannonball. She'd just see a blur in the distance. At that time I would turn around and laugh at her and say, "Come on, kid, you can do better than that."

Corker was still standing in the doorway, and it was out of character for her to just stand around. I wondered what she wanted.

"Did you like the movie?" she asked Joshua, who was hanging over the edge of the couch with a Golden Book in his hands.

"Uh-huh!" Joshua exclaimed.

"I did too!" added Miggie Thompson, who lived three houses down the street and who was on the floor writing me a "letter" on a scratch pad.

"The whole neighborhood had to go," I complained. *Everyone but Darlene,* I thought. "Ten kids in a Volkswagen Rabbit," I continued. "Boy, did I have a headache! How was *your* movie?" Corker and Steve had decided to go see some kind of a German movie at the last minute. They had unusual taste in movies, I thought. Not only that, but they liked to do other things that seemed unusual — like looking for old books in strange shops, or visiting museums, art galleries, and foreign restaurants. They also liked seminars, and they liked just driving around Salt Lake looking at things.

"Our movie was fun," Corker replied, and her eyes lit up for a minute. But then they dimmed. I should have realized that she needed to talk, especially when she asked her next question in a quiet voice. "How did you like Steve's homecoming yesterday?"

"What? Speak up."

"How did you like Steve's homecoming," she said, with a little more oomph.

I nodded. "Didn't do a bad job, did he?" In truth, Steve had done an outstanding job. I could see now why he had hesitated to tell his experiences before. They weren't the kind you wanted to use as small talk. "I guess you were probably the only one who understood the German part, huh? I mean, when he bore his testimony in German?"

"Yes." Corker had a funny look on her face which verified my assumption that the testimony had been meant for her. Then she sighed heavily. "He's so committed."

"So what else is new?" I asked, switching the channel again. Had I used my head, or should I say, my heart, I would have clicked off the TV, but I wasn't using either. I wasn't thinking about Corker's dilemma and the fact that she really didn't have anyone to talk to. Her best friend, Cynthia Trigger, had gone to summer school at UCLA, and her other friend, Trudy Amhurst, was staying in Chicago with her dad. But I didn't think about that. I was too busy. I was watching "The Price Is Right."

"Alfreda McGlockin! Come on down!" the announcer shouted, and I grinned as Alfreda, a middle-aged hausfrau type, bounced down the aisle hysterically waving her arms. I hardly heard Corker's next question.

"Ben?"

"Huh?" I took a big bite of the scrambled egg that had been waiting for me on the television. Then I picked up a piece of cantaloupe.

"I have a question."

"Shoot!"

"Have you ever wondered if you would love your kids?"

"Nope," I said, swallowing the piece of cantaloupe and wiping my mouth on my pajama sleeve.

"No, I guess you haven't. I don't know why I'd be asking you a dumb question like that," she said, looking at Joshua and Miggie. "You've always liked kids — all kids."

I ruffled Joshua's hair. "Whatever makes you think that? I can't help it if they're always hanging around here." Alfreda had won an electric guitar and had a chance to win a motorcycle. "All right!" I exclaimed. When I looked back, Corker was gone. I shrugged, and without taking my eyes off the TV I stepped back up on my mini-tramp because I wondered if I could do fifty more jumps.

That night I heard them from the kitchen. Terms like *male chauvinist* and *women's libber* were flipping out of our living room like rubber bands. I had just come home from the bindery, and I couldn't believe what I was hearing. The lovers were having a row, and it sounded like a bad one—a real argument, not just a little lovers' spat. It was the ugly, name-calling, serious type of argument, and I seemed to be hearing the middle of it.

"Oh, yes, and your mother, your dear mother, Devoted Dora Domestic," I heard Corker say in a tone that made even me mad. "Her entire life has been devoted to family—cooking, sewing, slaving her life away."

"How did my mother get into this?" Steve asked.

Yes, I said to myself, *how did Frances get into this?*

"Well, isn't she typical . . . the typical—?"

"She likes to take care of the people she loves," Steve interrupted. "Is that what you mean? She likes to cook for people, for instance. But then, anybody can like to cook if they want to learn to like to cook, if they let themselves. *You* could put a little more effort into liking it, you know, but you're so opposed to liking anything that remotely resembles . . ."

Don't say anything about cooking, Steve, I thought. *I wouldn't mention that, if I were you.*

". . . resembles domesticity, or anything associated with it. You certainly wouldn't want to be labeled as domestic. Tell me. Why? Why, when you were born a woman?"

"Oh, I see, and a woman is for cooking, huh? Yes, cooking, slaving, bowing down to the royal king—her husband! Well, let me tell you something. I was born a person like you, and I have every right to—"

"You have every right and an obligation to fulfill your destiny. A woman should—"

"Here we go again!" Corker was almost shouting. "A woman should, a woman should. And since when are you an authority on what a woman should do? Have you ever been one? Do you have the slightest idea what it's like to be a woman? You think all a woman is good for is service, slavery—"

"I never said—"

"No, but you implied it. You'll expect your wife to be just like your mother—a sweet Cinderella. Yes, the joke's on Cinderella—all the Cinderellas in the world. Cinderella marries her prince charming, and guess what? He takes her to the palace and says, 'Oh by the way, my dear, let me show you to the royal kitchen. It's all yours.' Well, I'm sorry, but that isn't for me. I need to be somebody. I need to prove to myself that—"

"Yes, Corker, what exactly are you trying to prove? That you aren't feminine? That you're tough? That you have no heart? Well, you *are* feminine, very feminine, and I happen to know you have a heart. You're also vulnerable. So vulnerable it's pathetic. Don't you see, I want to protect you . . . I—"

"Don't touch me! I don't need anyone's protection. Leave me alone! Go home and protect your mother!"

"My mother again, huh? Is it really so hard for you to believe that maybe, just maybe, she enjoys what she does?"

"I think she's been brainwashed."

"Why? Because she isn't the modern woman who is out to please only herself? The modern woman who is out for her own selfish—"

"That's right! I won't be a doormat! If that's selfishness, then I'm selfish and proud of it."

"What makes you think anyone's trying to walk on you?"

"I don't want to talk to you anymore, Steve, because it's obvious by now that we have nothing whatsoever in common!" The door slammed, and the next thing I knew, Corker was in the kitchen.

"Great!" Steve shouted after her. "Run away from yourself, run away from your feelings. That's always the easiest way out, isn't it?"

Her eyes were wild and she glared at me. "And you too!" she said. "You're nothing but a male chauvinist."

"What did I do?" I asked. "I'm just sitting here finishing off my cantaloupe."

"Just leave me alone!" she shouted, and her face became contorted and she stormed out of the kitchen.

"All right! All right!"

But I shouldn't have left her alone. I should have gone upstairs and talked to her then. Instead I clicked on the kitchen TV. *It's best not to get involved,* I thought. *It's her life.* And I tried to forget about what had just happened. It wasn't my life, and it was none of my business. I didn't go into the living room and talk to Steve either, although I knew he was still there. Finally I heard the front door close quietly.

Corker left early the next day. She had packed her things during the night and made several phone calls. Mom stayed home from work and cried a lot, and I sat watching TV numbly. I didn't want to think about what had just happened. But when Steve stopped by about nine-thirty, I had to think about it. He seemed to know before I told him. Maybe he could tell by my face. I've never been very good with bad news. "She's gone," I said. "She took off for New York like a shot about six-thirty this morning. She took a cab to the airport. Do you want to sit down?" He looked sick.

"Thanks." Our easy chair swallowed him up, just as it swallows everyone up. "Same old man-eating chair," I joked. But of course he didn't laugh. Instead he put his head in his hands. When he finally looked up, his face looked even worse. I'm not an M.D., but I knew enough to know that he was feeling rotten.

"It's my fault," he said. "I don't know why I said some of those stupid things. What do I care if she doesn't know how to cook, or even if she hates it. I know how to cook a little. I could have helped in the kitchen. And she wouldn't have needed to be domestic. We could have hired somebody. I did the wash on my mission . . . sorted all my own socks . . . I only lost a couple of socks the whole two years. I should have told her it didn't matter. But when she said that about my mother, I reacted. So what if my mother's domestic? She likes it. I shouldn't have acted like being domestic was some kind of a commandment."

"Aw, come on, Steve," I said, trying to help him feel better. "I don't think she left because of what you said. She's had her bags packed for quite a while. She's just been waiting for an excuse. It's something in her. She was born with it, I think. She's just always wanted to be top—big time, you know that. She thinks she's going to New York and make a million, get a posh apartment; show the world at last that she's somebody. She's always wanted to be important, and she's been talking about New York since she was fourteen. She talked about being a corporate executive at first, and then she just talked about being big time in the fashion business. The top, always the top. Maybe it was best she left, for you, anyway. For Corker, I don't know." I sighed and wondered why I was talking so much. "I think she was afraid of herself around you, and maybe afraid of you — or what you represent, anyway."

"Why?"

I shrugged. "Maybe she was afraid she wouldn't measure up. Or maybe . . . Oh, I don't know."

"Yes, and I didn't help any, did I?" He hit the chair with his fist.

"Careful, it deflates," I said. But my jokes weren't getting a lot of laughs. "Besides . . ." I paused. "Never mind, let's just say she left because she wanted to be somebody, and leave it at that. I don't want to get into any analytical stuff."

"What?"

"Oh, nothing. Let's just forget it." I was wishing I hadn't said anything, wishing I had just stayed uninvolved.

I sat down on the couch. Foxtrot jumped up onto my lap. "Okay, it's just that Corker wasn't sure she wanted kids. Some people really don't like kids, you know." I looked down at Foxtrot. "Some cats don't either, do they, Foxtrot? Foxtrot had kittens when we were little kids. Corker and I were pretty excited. But Foxtrot decided it was a good time for a little vacation and left the little critters mewing for their lives just two days after they were born. We thought she'd been hurt or run over or something, and we looked for her until late that night with flashlights. We fed the kittens with Corker's old doll bottles and an eye dropper. Foxtrot came home three days later as if nothing was wrong. Corker couldn't believe it. She kept saying 'She never loved them. She never even loved them.' Corker couldn't get over that." And I muttered, "Dumb cat!"

"But what does that have to do with Corker. She's not a cat. She's a person . . . a woman. It's a totally different thing."

I shrugged again. "It just bothered her," I said. "Then, of course, there was the babysitting. Guess how many times she went babysitting?" I held up my index finger. "Once. They had five kids in a two-bedroom university village apartment. The kids screamed the whole time. She said it was the worst experience she'd ever had, and she never went again. And . . . I don't suppose it helped any that kids were always hanging around here — squirting our hose, getting into our things, sometimes even crawling in the windows. I suppose I'm a Pied Piper of sorts. Anyway, Mom always told her 'When it's your own, it's different.' Corker would say 'Yes, but how do you know that for sure until it's too late.' So, anyway, she didn't know if she could love her own little kid, see?"

"I know. I know. She mentioned it. I know. But maybe we wouldn't have needed to have kids. Not everybody has kids."

"Come on, Steve!" I half-laughed. Now he was getting pathetic. "Don't give me that baloney. You're crazy about kids. So don't try to tell me you'd be happy not going for the family plan. You're the family-man type. Your bumper sticker even says so: 'Happiness is being a family.' Now, that's not exactly a macho bumper sticker. So don't give me that, okay?" Steve looked as if he was going to cry.

"You're right." He put his head in his hands again. "So tell me something. Why do I love her? Why can't I get a stupor of thought or something?"

"A what?"

"A stupor of thought . . . D&C 9:9. Why didn't I forget her on my mission?"

"Cheer up, old buddy, maybe you can still get that stupor of thought or whatever it's called. There's always hope."

Steve stared straight ahead, then looked at the pictures of Corker on the mantel. "Maybe," he said. I followed his eyes to the pictures which showed Corker in various stages of growing up.

I could feel Steve's misery, but I was feeling plenty of my own. Mine was mostly made up of guilt. Hadn't Dad asked me to look after Corker? Not long before he died he said, "I know it'll be hard, but try to look after her, Son." Then he winked. "And good luck!" But had I helped her? Had I looked after her? No. I had played a part, a big part, in Corker's anti-domestic behavior. Every time she tried to do something in the kitchen, I had made her feel like a fool. Cooking was the one lousy thing I could do better than she could; the one lousy thing! And it made me feel good to bang away at her self-esteem. That's where Steve and I differed. His masculine ego didn't rely on being better than somebody else. He was totally secure. But I was so insecure I had to rely on cooking. What am I saying? Am I saying that cooking helped my masculine ego? Yes, I guess I am.

Steve stood up, looking like misery personified. "I'll go home," he said. And a few seconds later the screen door slammed.

I hit the arm rest. *Life is the pits,* I thought.

That night, after I finished at the bindery, I tried to read the paper and I tried to work on the term paper that had been due three months ago, and I tried to watch TV. But I couldn't even concentrate on the show. I kept thinking about my sister and the part I had played in her life. I couldn't seem to get my mind in gear, and I couldn't seem to forget it. I had been a lousy brother. Why hadn't I talked to her more? Why hadn't I been there when she needed me? Now she was alone in New York.

I found a pencil and a piece of paper in the desk, and I began scrawling down some words. I told her about Steve's misery. "He still loves you," I wrote. I told her I was sorry I had always made fun of her. I said it was my fault she had left. But when I read it over, the words didn't sound the way I wanted them to sound. The letter sounded insipid. And it didn't matter, because I didn't know where to send it anyway. And the thought came to me to pray for Corker instead.

It's ironical that the first real prayer I ever offered, I mean the first prayer that was sincere enough to make it past the ceiling, was for someone else—ironical, because selfishness was my middle name. The prayer was short and to the point.

"You hear a lot of bad things about New York," I said. "I'm not sure, because I've never been there, and maybe the people who live there don't think it's so bad, but, well, I've heard about the mugging and the porn. Could you please keep Corker away from anything bad over there? Now, Corker likes to be independent. Well, yeah, of course you know that, you know everything. But, if there's any way, could you please keep her off Times Square."

Just then I heard Mom's footsteps clicking down the stairs to my room.

"Corker sent a telegram. Ben! She's okay. She's staying at Blaycocks and she's fine. Oh, I'm so relieved."

"Oh, good," I said. Then I remembered my prayer. *Never mind,* I said nonverbally. *She seems to be all right. Sorry I bothered you.* Mom handed me the telegram. *"Will send letter soon. Don't worry. Staying at Blaycocks. Will love New York. I'm fine."*

I read through the paper a couple of times. *Well, New York,* I thought, *watch out for my sister. She's a corker.* But I felt a little funny inside — guilty and empty, almost as if I missed my sister. Corker was such a presence. Not having her around would be dreary. We had never been separated before, except for a week I went camping with the Morgans and the few days every summer she stayed with Aunt Myrtle in Sacramento. I was twenty-three years old and I was missing my baby sister. That's being real tough, isn't it! Real macho!

6

It didn't take many letters from Corker to convince me that there was no need to worry about my baby sister in New York —nor did there seem to be any reason for me to wallow in misery or guilt. Corker, as usual, had planned carefully and was executing that plan with precision. In a matter of days she had landed a sales clerking and part-time modeling job in what she termed an "exclusive" women's clothing shop. The owner, she also mentioned, happened to be a friend of Lillian, the famous fashion mogul. I wondered how on earth Corker had found out that tidbit of information, but it didn't surprise me that she knew and it didn't surprise me that she was still aiming for the top.

Mom sighed as she finished reading the last letter from Corker. She took off her glasses and placed them on the TV. "I guess I was hoping she'd hate New York and be home right away," said Mom. "But, as usual, she's thriving."

"Maybe she'll hate it later," I said soothingly. "Maybe she hasn't had time to hate it yet. Who knows." I was jogging on my mini-trampoline again and I was up to 482.

"Why do you always have to be jogging on that thing?" Mother snapped then. It was obvious that she was taking her disappointment out on me. "I can't have a decent conversation with you anymore because you're always going up and down, down and up. It's hard to look into a person's eyes when he keeps moving up and down. You feel like you're following the bouncing ball."

"After D-Day I'll sit still for you. I'll look you right in the eye when you talk to me," I said. "You'll have my undivided attention."

"What's D-Day?" she asked.

"Darlene-day," I said. "The big moment when I sprint past the sprinter."

"I see. Well, good luck," my mother said unhappily.

I knew she needed to talk about Corker, but I was once again playing ostrich when it came to the subject of Corker. I was concentrating instead on training my body. The one aim in my life at present was to get into good enough shape to race past Darlene Morgan. And the target date was nearing. I read affirmation cards as I jogged. "I am strong! I am a winner! I have power! I can do anything!"

I was still trying to convince myself of my own prowess two weeks later when D-Day arrived. "I can do anything!" I said, as I gobbled down a huge breakfast rich in carbohydrates to give me energy. "I can beat Darlene!" I looked out of the kitchen window and added, "even in the rain." I didn't wonder whether Darlene would jog this morning, because something told me that Darlene was as dependable as the mail. The sprinting must go through!

I was just beginning to get fidgety when Darlene made her appearance. She was adequately dressed in a blue plastic rain thing of some kind, and as she tucked a few escaping wisps of her golden brown hair under the cap, my heart began beating rapidly. I told myself it was beating in anticipation of the big race, but in all probability it was beating at the sight of Darlene. My stomach also felt a little funny until I forced myself to remember her infamous words: "three-hundred-pound weakling." Instantly I felt strengthened, and revenge filled my chest cavity. "I'll get you for that, baby," I muttered. "Three-hundred-pound weakling, huh?" My nostrils flared like an angry bull's.

As Darlene started down the driveway, I began counting. I had decided to give her an extra hundred counts so that I could pass her on even sidewalk. But I was only on number fifty-three when Mom groped her way into the kitchen and saw me waiting to go out. She seemed to awaken immediately. "You're not going out like that?" she said. "Son, it's raining." My mother has poor timing when it comes to asserting her motherliness.

I raised my hand to indicate that I was counting — "fifty-eight . . . fifty-nine . . ."

Mother quickly opened the bottom drawer near the fridge, ransacked through it, and pulled out some plastic bags. "Let me cut these for you. I could cut a face out of this small one and you can slip this old cleaner's bag over your clothes."

"Nah, I'll be fine," I said. "Ninety-eight . . . ninety-nine . . . a hundred!"

"But, Ben," Mom said, trying to lasso me with the plastic bag. "Here. Please. For me!"

"Let go!" I said, pulling away from her. "Don't you know you're never supposed to give your children plastic bags? I'm fine. Good-bye, Mother." I tried to pull away from her. "Now quit it, Mom. It's D-Day. Go back in the house," I added, as she followed me out of the door in a last attempt to get the cleaning bag over me.

"Ben," she shouted after me. "You'll catch cold. Please, honey." I hoped Darlene couldn't hear her.

I hit the sidewalk and saw Darlene lobbing a few houses ahead of me at an easy pace. I checked behind me to make sure Mom wasn't still following me and then I began concentrating on catching up with Darlene. My heart began thumping faster and faster as I got closer and closer. The rain was also thumping faster and faster, and raindrops pelted my face and T-shirt. But it didn't matter, because I was almost up with Darlene. I had just a few more sloshy steps to go.

"Good grief, Ben! You're going to catch a cold," Darlene said, as I caught up with her. I noticed that the rain was making her eyelashes thick and even darker than usual. "You'd better go back and get something to protect yourself."

"Don't worry about me," I said roughly, as I licked a little rain from my lips. It irked me that conversation had made the moment less meaningful. I had planned so carefully how I would say the words "You can do better than that, kid." Now I had to change the wording a little. "Don't worry about me, worry about yourself, kid," I said. "You can do better than that, can't you?"

By the time I had said it, however, I was a little further ahead of her than I had planned — and I was also more out of breath than I had planned to be. I realized that all my pauses to gasp for breath had robbed the statement of impact. But I was sure Darlene would accept my challenge, and I began running like crazy. When I glanced behind me, Darlene was still running casually. By this time I was really gasping, and I could do nothing but slow down. When I looked behind me again, Darlene was gradually moving closer. To my horror, she seemed to be catching up effortlessly, calmly. With huge sighs of breath, I forced my legs to move, but I must not have been moving quickly, because it didn't take Darlene more than a few seconds to catch up with me.

"I'm sorry, Ben," she said, smiling pleasantly. "I didn't hear what you said just now. I guess because of the rain. I just heard something about doing better."

"Never mind," I said, sloshing through the puddles, hoping to get reheated for one last time, hoping that the adrenaline would save me and spark the failing engine once again. I forced myself to leap ahead of her with one last springing effort, but she caught up with me easily again. By now I was feeling nauseous and my left side throbbed.

"Ben, you look bad. Are you feeling all right?"

"Don't worry about me," I said, hissing like a steam engine.

"Well, I *am* worried. Please turn back, and walk home," she pleaded, with sincere concern in her voice.

"I can't," I answered.

"Why not?"

I hesitated because I was ready to collapse. My stomach was in my throat. "Because . . . because I don't think I can even walk," I admitted, as I sank to the wet lawn. I was too ill to be embarrassed.

"Come on, get up, I'm not leaving you out here to drown," Darlene said, trying to lift me by the armpits.

"I can't," I moaned.

"Come on" she persisted until I let her help me up.

Ten minutes later Darlene turned me over to my mother,

who instantly put milk on the stove to warm, pulled out my red, white, and blue flag pajamas from the drier and put a towel on my head. Darlene waved good-bye rather sweetly and compassionately. "I'll check on you later," she said. "I still have a mile or two to go." She tried not to smile at my "King Tut" look.

"I still have a mile or two to go," I repeated nasally after she had left.

"Now, Ben," Mom said. "Just be glad Darlene's taken life-saving."

When Darlene stopped by later that morning, I didn't come out of the TV room.

"You okay, Ben?" she called.

"He's still in his pajamas," I heard Mom say. "I really think he's coming down with something."

"I'm not coming down with anything," I shouted. "Cool it, Mom."

"Okay, Ben, if you say so," Mom called back.

"Are you sure you're okay," Darlene repeated loudly.

"Look, I'm fine. Just fine, okay? I'm a big, strong boy."

"Okay," she said. "See you around. I just wanted to check on you."

I could hear Darlene and Mom talking about me then, and at last I could hear Darlene getting ready to leave. "Hey, Darlene, do you play Ping-Pong?" I asked.

"Yes, a little. Why?"

It scared me the way she said "Yes, a little." *Like she jogs a little?* I wondered.

"Why?" she repeated. "Do you want a game a little later?"

"Not today," I said. "Maybe later." I thought she had sounded too eager.

My emotionally depleting D-Day caused me to work more slowly at the bindery that evening. The physical strain of the morning hadn't helped either. It was late when I tiptoed into the TV room and turned on the television quietly. There was nothing on but the channel number, so I turned it back off and decided to eat away my disappointment. As I opened the fridge, I noticed the last letter from Corker, lying on the counter next to it. I hadn't read it yet, and I picked it up and skimmed through the first three pages quickly while I fixed myself a piece of toast and strawberry jam. But when I saw the name "Lillian" I backed up.

I knew who she was the minute I saw her. Lillian is extremely small and much older than her pictures. Her eyes pierce through you when she gives you the privilege of looking at you. I saw her wandering around the shop looking at things. Apparently she had just had coffee with Jack and he had gone to get something to show her. *It's now or never*, I thought. I admit I was a little scared, but I walked right up to her and introduced myself. She said, "What do you want?" And I answered, "I'd like to work for you. That's why I came to New York. It was impossible to get an interview with your people and I thought maybe—"

"We're not hiring," she interrupted.

Her curtness stunned me, and I tried to get my thoughts reorganized. "When do you think you *will* be hiring?" I asked.

She sighed at my persistence. "Quite frankly, you're too short for a top modeling job, dear," she said.

"I'm not interested in modeling," I answered. "Modeling doesn't last. I'm looking for a career."

I guess all girls want to model, so that got her attention. "My, aren't you ambitious." Then she frowned. "And what makes you think you'd be qualified to work for me?" she asked.

"I'm very well prepared. I've been planning this for years."

"Oh?" But then she looked at my hopeful face and it probably looked like all the other hopeful faces. "There are fifty thousand girls out there who would like to work for me," she said. "You're not so different."

"Yes, I am. Would you like to see my resumé?"

"Not particularly," she said. But I pretended she hadn't said it and I ran to my counter where it was waiting and I had it back in her hands in about fifteen seconds. "My, aren't you efficient?" Her voice sounded tired and she looked around to see if Jack might be coming yet to rescue her. He wasn't, so she thumbed through the pages pretending to be reading them. But then, just before she closed it, she must have noticed my underlined statement: *French — Fluently.* "You speak French a little?"

"*Mais oui,*" I said, showing off like Miss Piggy. I told her then — in French, of course — how much I wanted to work for her. I rambled on for a full two minutes. I could tell she was impressed, and in fact she was excited. Few people know about Lillian's French background, because she refuses to talk about it.

"You speak French very well. How long did you live there?"

"I've never been to France, but I started speaking French in sixth grade and I've always loved it."

"Oh, I see." She seemed disappointed that I wasn't French, and she handed back my resume. "Very nice," she said. "But I can't hire every girl who speaks French fluently." She glanced in the direction of Jack's office and I could see it was my last chance to make an impression, because Jack was heading toward us.

"My nickname is Corker," I said quickly. "And that's because I *am* a corker. I'm quick and capable. The difference between me and the fifty thousand others who would like to work for you is that you need me."

She did a double take and lifted her eyebrows. Then she looked amused. "My, aren't you arrogant?" she said. "Arrogant and egotistical! Jack, darling, this is simply elegant," she said, making a fuss over a new gown Jack had draped over his arm. Lillian didn't look at me again, not even when she left. But that afternoon — you won't believe this — but that afternoon I was shocked to receive a call from Lillian's secretary. She suggested I be in the office at two o'clock sharp. Needless to say I was there early. Lillian's office is absolutely huge, and Lillian looked tiny and pruneish behind the monstrous desk.

"Well, Corker," she said quietly. "Have a seat. Do you know why you're here?"

"Because I'm arrogant?" I asked.

She smiled then. "Exactly," she said. "I happen to be extremely arrogant myself and very difficult to get along with."

"I've read about that," I answered.

"But arrogance doesn't mean anything unless you are also capable and talented." She was frowning again, and she turned over some kind of an egg timer. "You have exactly five minutes to tell me why I need you."

I began talking fast. But then I've always been a fast talker. I talked so quickly about my education, my background, my goals, that I was out of breath when the five minutes were up. She just sat there looking at me until a small smile crept to her lips. Then she looked out of her window and seemed to be in another world for a full two minutes or so. At last she came to, and she pushed a buzzer on her desk. "Janet, show Corker around, please. She's going to be working with us."

"Thank you!" I almost shouted. But I remembered my old job. "Oh, but I . . . I really should . . ."

"Don't hum and haw, dear. If it's Jack you're worried about, he'll be absolutely thrilled at his good taste."

Later that day Lillian gave me some clues about what she had in mind for me. It sounds like some kind of a French connection—a girl-Friday type job. I'm not sure even *she* knows what I'll be doing, but apparently it's important because she wants me to move into a posh penthouse right away. She says she pays her employees "very well" and she wants them to live like she pays them well. She also mentioned casually that she expects total commitment and total brain power and effort. "Some days you'll be so tired, you won't know who you are," she said. "Just be prepared for a lot of pressure. You'll work like you've never worked before."

"I'm not afraid of hard work," I said, and she liked that.

As I folded the letter, I wondered how Corker could have known in sixth grade that she would need French someday. Then I frowned at another thought: Steve. I would have to tell him the bad news. *Why can't Corker just be a normal, everyday girl who gets homesick and comes home,* I wondered. *Why does she always have to be unusual? And why was I blessed with such a wonder for a sister.* The vision of myself being carried home by Darlene that morning flashed through my mind. *Isn't it wonderful that Corker is making a name for herself in New York, while I'm making a fool of myself in Salt Lake City?* I thought. Self-disgust made me throw down the letter and slam the fridge door against the cabinets, making the smaller bottles in the door rattle. I opened the produce drawer with a jerk and noticed it was packed with grapes. Apparently Mom had come across a good buy. After I had eaten several pounds of them I went to bed and wondered if grapes can ferment once they're inside the human body. When I finally got to sleep, I dreamed that I was a huge grape in a Fruit-of-the-Loom commercial.

I wasn't sure why I was awake at six-thirty the next morning until I heard the tapping against the window. I rubbed my eyes and stumbled out of bed, holding my pajamas closed where the button had popped. With squinting eyes, I opened the curtain. I should have recognized the jogging shoes, but I looked up at her from my basement window and felt like Jack of Jack and the Bean Stalk fame, looking up at the giant. She kneeled down, and her clear eyes and wide Pepsodent smile almost blinded me. "Good morning," she said, too cheerfully. If there's one thing I can't stand it's people who can say "good morning" cheerfully, and I frowned at her.

"What do you want?" I growled through the slightly open window.

"I came to see if you wanted to jog this morning with me. It's a lot easier to get out when you have somebody to talk to. And I brought you my running book. Have you read it yet?"

"No," I moaned. "And I'm not interested. I didn't get to bed till late."

"Oh, I'm sorry I woke you up then. Are you sure you don't want to come? Well, maybe tomorrow. Go back to bed." But I didn't do what she suggested, because her smile had partially awakened me. When Darlene started doing some warming-up exercises, I really began waking up.

"What are you doing?"

"Stretching," she replied.

"Oh." I kept watching her, mesmerized. "Well," I said. "Maybe I could go after all, if I did that first." I liked the way Darlene stretched. "Can you wait a minute?" I rushed into the bathroom, brushed my teeth, combed my hair, threw on my clothes, and hoped she wouldn't notice my whiskers and blood-shot eyes. It did take me an extra few seconds to comb through my moustache.

"Now tell me about stretching," I said, as the fresh morning air smacked me in the face. "And . . . let me see you do that again."

"People who are serious about running try to limber up first," she said, as she stretched her leg.

"Oh, I see," I said, as I watched her.

"Come on, you do it," she continued, when she noticed I was just standing there watching her. So I stretched myself a little.

"Does this help you run faster?" I asked.

"Yes, if you want to run faster, but you're not out to run faster, really. You don't want to deplete your strength right off the bat. You just want to run a nice even pace to get your heart beating faster, and yet you don't want to run so quickly that you're totally wiping yourself out. I think your mistake has been that you've been trying to out-do yourself."

"I thought we were supposed to do that, coach," I said. "I thought a guy was supposed to give it everything he's got."

She began running slowly, and I followed her example. "We can run at a nice conversational pace and talk while we do it. Interested?" She smiled again.

"Sure," I answered, as I caught up with her. I couldn't help noticing once again how clear and light her eyes were. But then she ruined the moment by talking. I didn't like what she was saying.

"Ben, I hope it doesn't bother you that I've been running a little longer and can outrun you a little."

I didn't answer. I just grunted.

"It doesn't, does it? Because it shouldn't."

Oh yeah, sure, I thought. *Me man, you woman. Me strong, you puny.*

"Let me tell you why it shouldn't matter."

"Are you going to preach?"

"Yes."

"Okay, just so I know. I can be prepared. Do you need a pulpit to preach your women's lib stuff?"

"No, I can just preach while I'm running, I think. And it isn't women's lib stuff."

"What is it then?"

"Just a philosophy. It's just this. We're all different, and where I am may be different than where you are, but it doesn't matter as long as we're both trying to be better. Right? All that counts is that we're both moving along our own roads of progression."

"I look at it as a ladder—a ladder of success or progression," I said, putting in my two cents' worth.

"Okay, we're all climbing different ladders of progression then."

"I certainly hope so. Can you see thousands of people trying to climb the same ladder."

"The point is—"

"Darlene," I interrupted, "that's a very nice philosophy."

"Thanks," she said. "I'm glad you like it."

"Darlene," I said again.

"Yes?" she asked, surprised that I had more to say.

"I'm still going to cream you someday."

"That's fine, Ben," she said. I guess she could see that I hadn't understood the point she was trying to make, because she changed the subject and asked how Corker was doing. So far I wasn't enjoying our conversation.

"Speaking of running," I said, "my sister always runs fastest when she's running away from herself. I guess we could call her the unsinkable Corker Van Vleet."

"So you think she'll be staying, huh?"

"No chance of her coming home now. She's in cahoots with that big wheel, Lillian. She's assistant or something."

"Not *the* Lillian. You're kidding."

"*The* Lillian, the millionairess."

"How did she do it?" Darlene asked in awe.

"Who knows," I answered. "You know Corker."

"She's really something, isn't she? Who else could pull something like that off in less than a month?" She was quiet then and looked concerned. "I wish Steve were doing as well," she said softly. "I'm awfully worried about him. He isn't himself. He's been moping around since she left. Thank goodness school starts soon. I hope he can concentrate on it."

"There's always another bus," I said. "Steve just needs a good substitute girl friend and he'll be just fine."

"I hope so. But it's been quite a while and he's still . . . Well, this news is going to set him back even further, I'm afraid."

"Guess you'll be telling him, huh?" I asked hopefully.

"Guess I'll have to," she said.

Good, I thought. *Then I won't have to.*

A few minutes later, Darlene looked at me carefully. "Oh dear, I think you ought to go back now, Ben." I guess she could see that I was struggling to keep going.

"I can make it," I said, feeling anger at her motherly attitude. "I think I can keep up with a puny person like you."

"For Pete's sake, Ben! I've been running for over two years. Remember — different ladders?"

I nodded. I was beginning to feel sick and I *wanted* to turn around.

"Please, Ben, do it for me."

"You talked me into it," I said, with jerks in my voice. "But I'm still going to cream you one of these days."

She smiled sweetly and touched my arm. "Give yourself another couple of weeks and you probably will."

I felt defeated once again as I walked home. *A person can do anything,* I said to myself. *But why does it have to take so long.*

---- 7 ----

"You're a winner, Ben!" Darlene was patting me vigorously on the back. "You did it!"

"Oh, it was nothing really," I said, giving her the "tell me more" sign with my hand. It was the first time I had run the full distance to the chapel and back. I had progressed from being a three-hundred-pound-weakling to being a winner — a three-mile winner. True, I still had a few pounds to lose, but success breeds success and I was swiftly moving up the ladder to physical fitness.

It really wasn't difficult to succeed, with a long-legged beauty named Darlene as a running partner. Darlene made it easy to get out of the sack. No longer did I feel any need to compete with her, and I had long since forgiven her for her uncomplimentary and impulsive comment about me. Darlene was now my coach and my personal cheerleader, and it's difficult to feel bitterness for long toward your cheerleader. Like her brother, Darlene delighted in the accomplishments of others.

I have often wondered how the Morgans instilled in their children the desire not only to succeed themselves but to help others do the same. But then, I heard it often in the Morgan home: "You did great! Good job!" Encouragement is the word, I believe. The Morgans enjoyed seeing progress made by anyone and everyone. Even after I had creamed Darlene three times playing table tennis, and then two more times to make my point, she hadn't shown the slightest hint of poor sportsman-ship. And she had really tried to win. Darlene had only laughed happily and commented with respect for superior skill. "Hey, you're pretty good!" She and Steve were indeed a lot alike.

Now she was beside herself with excitement not at her own success but at my success in running three miles for the first time. "Hey, don't hit me so hard!" I said, as I half-laughed. "What are you, some kind of a heavy? Take it easy on an old man." I was still trying to get my breathing back to normal, because the last half mile had been difficult. Then I looked at her out of the corner of her eye and asked in between gasps, "Want to celebrate tonight? Go to a movie or something?" I skipped a gasp as I waited for her answer.

"A movie?" She seemed hesitant.

"Busy, huh?" I happened to know that Darlene wasn't busy, and I was playing a game. Joshua, my informant, had reported that Bill Higgens had asked her out but had come down with the flu and had cancelled. I also happened to know that Darlene had lined Steve up with Suzee Smithson. My next suggestion, I knew, would be the clincher. "We could maybe double with Steve if we could talk him into getting a date. Maybe we could even line him up with someone."

Darlene smiled mysteriously and said what I felt sure she would say. "He's got a date. I wanted him to meet a really sweet friend of mine. She's a super girl, really fun, and easy to get along with. Well, you'll have to meet her. Sure, I could go. Why not?"

Yes, why not? I repeated to myself.

"Besides, we really *do* need to celebrate," she added. "I'm so proud of you."

"Aw, shucks, cut it out!" I said humbly.

I was grinning and humming happily as I came into the house, and Mom looked away from her pan of scrambled eggs for a minute. I grabbed her around the waist and twirled her through the kitchen. "La-de-da-de-da . . . tra-la-la. Come on, Mom, kick up your heels a little."

"Oh, you, cut it out. I'm late for work. So how come you're so darn happy?"

"Because I'm a winner, that's why," I said. "I'm your pro-verbial success story. I just ran three miles, and you can see I still

have energy to spare. Look at this King Kong chest."
"Ahahahahaha," I beat it in Tarzan fashion. "Mom, do you remember when all I had was ring around the belly? Ring around the belly!" I sang nasally, mimicking the commercial. "Now look at me. Look at these arms — these biceps." I pulled up my sleeve and flexed for her.

"You got those from running?" Mom asked, amazed.

"No, silly, of course not. I've been lifting some weights and some of the cans of food storage. I'm a winner, Mom. I'm tough. I'm rugged and I'm almost down to my perfect weight. Ahahahahah," I bellowed again.

Mom went back to her pan of eggs and only glanced back at me once more, quickly. "So what shirt will you need?" she asked.

"For what," I asked, dumbfounded.

"For the date you just got with Darlene," she said matter-of-factly.

That night, as Steve, Darlene, Suzee, and I perused the paper for a suitable movie, I could tell that Suzee Smithson was indeed easy to get along with; but then, we were all being easy to get along with — too easy to get along with.

"It doesn't matter to me. What do you want to see?"

"Have you seen *War in Space*?"

"Yes, but I really don't mind seeing it again. If that's what you guys would like to see, that's fine."

"Whatever the group wants, is fine with me too."

"It doesn't matter to me either. Anything's fine. I mean, if it's clean."

"Well, heck, why are we all being so nice?" I asked. "I'll tell you what I'd like to see. I'd like to see *Robin Hood* at the oldies but goodies theater place, because I'm broke and payday isn't until next Thursday. How does that sound?"

"That's fine," they all said, with obvious relief that somebody had made a decision.

It surprised me that Steve was so opinionless. He usually had a mind of his own. I realized as I continued observing him that he was floating through the evening just to get himself through. It was too bad, because Suzee Smithson wasn't bad. She had cute dimples, curly hair, and she even walked cute. She also obviously liked Steve, who hardly looked at her. I felt sorry for her. Steve wasn't trying to be rude. He was, in fact, trying to be extremely pleasant, but Suzee could tell. We could all tell that he still had Corker on the brain — or on the heart.

As the evening progressed, our group's ability to make decisions didn't improve. We had trouble deciding where to go get something to eat. We finally boiled it down to pizza or ice cream.

"It doesn't matter to me. I love both."

"Me too."

"Me too. Anything you guys would like is fine with me."

"Me too," I added, then I shook my head to rattle my brain a little. "Okay," I said, once again dribbling with the ball. "How does this sound?"

"That sounds great!" Suzee said it before I had finished.

"I haven't finished," I said.

"Oh, I'm sorry." She was a little embarrassed.

"Let's go get pizza and then stop for ice cream cones after." Somehow I knew they would all go for my idea. When I remembered my diet and my pocketbook, however, I wondered whether I should change my mind, but I didn't have the heart. So I suggested just a small pizza for a snack and then large ice-cream cones. I knew which girl at Bert's was the super-scooper.

"Does everyone like pepperoni?" I asked, as we sat around the table at Plus Pizza.

"Uh-huh, I love pepperoni," Darlene said.

"Fine with me," Steve said numbly.

"Anything you guys would like is fine. It doesn't matter to me," Suzee added.

I went ahead and ordered the pizza, and I noticed midway through her first piece that Suzee was removing the pieces of pepperoni and slipping them under her napkin. I felt sorry enough for her to order another pizza, mushroom this time, claiming I was still hungry. But, for myself, I ordered an extra large salad. The added order almost wiped out my pocketbook, but luckily Steve had extra.

Later that night, while Steve took Suzee home, I visited with Darlene in the Morgans' family room. I hoped my breath didn't smell like Roquefort, because I had plans. I sat down next to her on the couch but jumped back up to click on the television. I planned to lean down and kiss her during one of the commercials, and I stretched my hands and yawned. Darlene, I was sure, would be so overwhelmed by the charm and finesse of an older man that she'd be mine forever. There would be no more Bill Higgenses or Phil Blacks or Ralph Poplars or any other young bucks hanging around her place. There would be only one name in her little dating calendar book — mine.

The first commercial passed by uneventfully. During the second commercial I decided that, in order to kiss her, I would need to discuss something with her first. I doubted Darlene was the first-date-kisser type. "Darlene," I said, with masculine savvy. "I was just thinking that we've known each other for quite a few years, haven't we? I mean, it isn't as if this were really a first date. You and I have known each other and had fun times together for quite a while."

"Uh-huh," Darlene nodded. "I think I was only twelve, wasn't I, when you graduated from high school. Could that be right? My word! Hey, listen to this: I was just barely out of kindergarten when . . ."

"Never mind," I said, stretching my neck a little.

"Do you have a kink in your neck?"

That gave me an idea for a new angle. "No, but I think I'm getting one. Could you rub my neck right here?"

"Sure," Darlene said, and she massaged the area just above my right shoulder with her long slim fingers. "Does that feel any better?"

"Ah, does it ever!"

"Good." Darlene removed her hand and placed it in her lap. I looked at it for a while and then picked it up.

"Well, look what I found."

"My hand?" she asked calmly.

"Oh, is it? Well, my goodness, so it is! Look at that, I found your hand." I tickled her palm, and she looked at it and at me and then back at the television. I couldn't help noticing how soft her cheek looked in the light from the piano lamp. I touched her cheek, and when she didn't move away I turned her face toward mine and closed my eyes to lean down for what I planned would be the kiss of her lifetime.

"What are you doing," I mumbled through her hand.

66

"I just wanted to see how you would look without a moustache," she said.

"This isn't a good time to tell me you don't like my moustache," I said.

"I didn't say I don't like your moustache."

"You insinuated that you don't like my moustache. I happen to like it." I was getting miffed. My red moustache was a symbol of my masculinity, and I wasn't about to have anyone insult it. "Well, do you?" I asked anyway.

"What?"

"Do you like it?"

"Yes." She was quiet for a few seconds. "But it could use a little trim. So could your hair, for that matter."

"You're a fresh little squirt, aren't you."

"Don't call me a squirt," Darlene said. "It lacks respect. I'm sorry if I hurt your feelings, because I really didn't mean to."

"You just don't like my moustache."

"I did not say that, Ben." There was a long pause, because I was angry. Darlene decided to break the silence by rubbing my face in her insult. "Do you have trouble eating? I mean, getting food on it. I've always wondered if moustaches are a problem that way."

"Why, does it have mozzarella on it, or something?"

"No," she said. "Tomato sauce." I should have noticed the twinkle in her eye, but instead I quickly tried to groom my moustache, using my fingers as a comb.

"I'm just kidding," Darlene giggled. "You do that so funny. You look like a raccoon washing up."

"What, this?" I combed through my moustache again so that she would giggle again.

"Darlene, you know what I think," I asked suddenly, leaning down close to her face, my arm around her back. Her large blue eyes stared into mine without blinking, and I could smell Ivory soap on her face.

"No," she said softly, and I watched her lips form the O.

"I think you're really too young to kiss." I released her, moved away from her, and looked at her out of the corner of my eye.

Darlene didn't fall for my snare, and she began nodding

seriously. "Maybe you're right," she said. "I hadn't thought of that." Then she smiled the old Morgan grin.

"You're also clever for your age," I said.

We watched television for a while longer, but we weren't really watching it.

"You know what, Ben?" Darlene said.

"What?"

"I think you're an awfully nice person." I wondered what that was supposed to mean, and I waited for her to continue. She did. "But six o'clock is going to come very early tomorrow morning."

"Oh, brother, you want to go running tomorrow, huh?"

"Of course," she nodded.

"Of course," I mimicked.

"Ben, you know very well you like to run just as much as I do," she said. She was right and she knew she was right. I relished running now. It made me feel like a winner.

"You're right," I admitted. "If I'm planning to run a marathon or two next year, I can't quit now, can I."

"Nooooo," she said. "Not when you're doing so great." I watched a little sadly as she said "nooooo," and she laughed as I jumped up and started my stretching exercises. Somehow at this moment I didn't feel like a winner, and I was already looking forward to running again in the morning.

I couldn't get to sleep that night, and I got up and walked into the bathroom, turned on the light, and scrutinized my face in the medicine cabinet mirror. I turned my head from side to side. Darlene was right. My moustache was getting a little bushy. I trimmed it a little; then a little more — a hair here and a hair there. By the time I was finished there wasn't enough to leave, and my sideburns were getting long too, I decided. The next morning I shaved it all off — the moustache, the sideburns, the works. I felt like Samson, shorn of his strength because of a woman, and I stared at myself, embarrassed at what I had done and embarrassed to go outside and meet Darlene.

I waited so long that Darlene had to tap at our kitchen window. "Hurry, Ben, it's getting late," she called. I walked out sheepishly, but Darlene was starting down the driveway, and she didn't even look at me long enough to see the change.

"Steve didn't get in until two last night," she said as we ran. "I stayed up to talk to him, and I asked him how things went. Guess what he did."

"Hmmmm, I can't guess," I said, remembering how easy to get along with Suzee had seemed.

"Not what you're thinking," she said. "He drove Suzee home and then he drove around to all the places he and Corker used to visit—the museums, the restaurants, that dance place downtown, the—"

"That doesn't sound like a good way to get a stupor of thought, does it," I said.

"No," she agreed.

"I'll have to talk to him about it." I was feeling totally empathetic.

"I wish you would." Then she smiled. "You know what he said? He said that he thought maybe if he saturated himself he could get a stupor of thought."

"That doesn't make much sense, the poor looney bird." I stopped talking then, because I had no right to judge *him* for being a looney bird.

Darlene didn't even notice anything different about me until we were home. Suddenly she began laughing right in the middle of a sentence. "Ben. Hey, let me look at you! Ben, let me see." I must have blushed, because I could feel my face turning warm.

"I need a better hair cut," I said.

"But your face. Your moustache is gone. Your face—it's all nice and clean."

"It was clean before."

"I know. I know. But, Ben, you look fantastic."

"Yeah?" I said, looking up from the ground. "I was thinking I looked a lot better in my moustache."

"You looked awfully nice in your moustache," she said.

"I did? *Now* you tell me!"

"But, you know, I think you look even better without it," she added.

"I do, huh?"

"Yes, I'm glad you decided to shave it off."

What on earth could have prompted me? I thought.

"It's such a nice change," she said.

"You really like it then, huh?" I asked.

"Uh-huh!"

"Do you like being able to see my lips?"

She looked at my lips. "Yes," she said self-consciously. "They look fine." I leaned down and pulled her to me. Instantly, she put her hand over my mouth and grinned. "Let me see if I can remember how you looked *with* that moustache," she said. "Oh, yes, now I remember."

"That's what I figured," I complained. "You're fickle."

"And you, Ben," she giggled, "you're a pretty good friend. I'm glad you have a sense of humor."

I see, I thought sadly. *Friend.* The word bothered me a great deal, but I didn't show her it bothered me. "And you're one heck of a coach," I said, patting my stomach. There wasn't much left to pat.

8

Christmas always gets to me. It's a little embarrassing the way I start tingling inside just like a little kid when it approaches. But who can help getting excited at all the sights and sounds and smells and feelings — especially the feelings — of this best season of the year?

This Christmas wouldn't be quite like the others for Mom and me. Corker had written that she wouldn't be able to make it. She had some kind of a gala fashion show, plus several Christmas parties for a few small-time folks — some Congressmen and their wives; a movie star here and there; a prime minister or two; and, of course, some visiting royalty. "I can't possibly make it home," she had written. "Lillian is counting on me."

"Big-time bunk," I muttered, when Mom read me the letter. I felt bad for Mom, yet I couldn't help thinking that it might be best for Steve. He was finally getting involved in living again on a full-time scale. He was doing well in school and had a good part-time job as a bookkeeper. He was even beginning to get dates on his own without the help of Darlene or me. Seeing Corker could be a setback.

It was comforting to know that Mom and I still had our tried-and-true friends to rely on this Christmas. I had my fingers crossed that the Morgans would invite us over for Christmas dinner again this year. Maybe this time we could take them up on their offer. I'd help Frances and we'd put out something extra special. And for just one meal, I planned to stuff myself with whatever I wanted to eat: dressing, mashed potatoes with rich turkey gravy, hot buttered rolls. It would be my way of playing Santa Claus to myself for being such a good boy all year. So what if I had to run extra hard for a week or two afterwards? It would be worth it.

I was extremely proud of myself this Christmas. I looked good. I felt good. Self-mastery is a good feeling. I, Ben Van Vleet, was a healthy specimen: physically fit, strong, a winner! I had lost sixty pounds, and it was gratifying to try on my Santa Claus suit and find it bagging around the tummy area. Last year it had almost fit.

For the past five Christmases I had been asked to play Santa at the stake Christmas party. Every year I told them, "Hey, no thanks, get yourself another chump!" But every year they just figured I was kidding and they didn't bother to find a replacement. And so every year I played Santa. How could I let a hundred or so little kids down? Besides, I got a kick out of it, even if playing Santa wasn't the coolest thing to do. The previous year, Randy Winks had pulled off my white moustache, and when he saw my red one underneath he yelled out: "It's not Santa, it's Big Ben!" This year I wouldn't have the same problem—I didn't have a red moustache, and I planned to glue my white one on with something better; with super glue, or something like that.

I was a little out of practice with my "Ho-ho-ho's" this year, so I practiced while I got into my Santa suit. "Ho-ho-ho, boys and girls," I shouted, in my lowest voice. "And have you been good boys and girls this year?"

I pictured their faces and I couldn't help smiling. "Ho-ho-ho," I repeated until I thought I had it right. Then I hummed Christmas carols to myself. A half-hour later I was "just stuffed," but not with food this time—with a bed pillow and a sack of quilt batting. It was comforting to know that the stuffing wasn't my own.

Sister Ellis had said the goodies would be at the stake center and that all I needed to bring was Santa and his "Ho-ho-ho." I practiced again as I stepped out into the crisp December air. I was heading for the garage when Darlene came out to get the mail.

"Ho-ho-ho! It's Darlene Morgan," I said. "And have you been a good little girl this year, Darlene? Never mind, I know you have. I suppose you plan to go jogging on Christmas morning."

"Of course," she said. "But I'll wait until *after* I open my presents."

"Ah, the true spirit of Christmas," I said, with another "Ho-ho-ho."

As I started getting into my car, Darlene called out the same thing she always called out when I headed for my car: "Take a bike!"

"Very funny," I called back. "Santa on a bike."

But then I thought, *Why not?* It would set a good example, Santa doing something about his health and physical fitness. *Sure,* I thought. *I have time. I'm early. Why not?* Darlene grinned as I pulled my bike out of the garage and tucked my "stomach" behind the handlebars. Soon I, Santa Claus, was gliding down Vine Street. When I got to Ninth East, I really started getting some attention. I waved as I pedaled, and I got plenty of double takes.

"Hey, Santa, where's your sleigh?"

"Ho-ho-ho! No sleigh for me," I called back. "I'm into aerobics." When people rolled down their car windows I heard Christmas carols sounding from the radios. I saw some Christmas trees in trunks, and I noticed the decorations on the houses. It felt good to be out in the invigorating air, and it felt good to know that Christmas was approaching. Little children pressed their noses against the car windows, big-eyed, staring at Santa Claus on his bike. I waved at them, smiling as if I were in a parade. The air was clean, and my nose and cheeks would soon be as red as cherries; and that was fine, because that's the way Santa's cheeks and nose are supposed to look.

"Ho-ho-ho," I shouted again, and I waved at two dark-haired children who were jumping up and down in the back of a bus.

Then I heard someone scream.

I saw it first in my peripheral vision, and when I turned my head I saw that it was still coming. A truck, a yellow truck, was heading for me, crossing the middle section and lunging for me as if it had my number. "Hey!" I screamed. "Stop, you idiot!"

But it didn't stop. It sped closer, closer; growing larger, larger, until I could see the grille work and the headlights, looking like the face of a monster. I tried to turn and jump off my bike, but it was too late. The last thing I remember thinking was *Help me!*

I was floating down a long dark corridor toward an open door at the end. As I got closer to the light, I saw that the people were smiling beyond the door and it seemed to radiate peace. But I stopped myself, because I knew I wasn't ready to enter, and I began swimming, swimming the backstroke; and then I was riding my bike; and then I was running . . . running down the corridor. I was panting and gasping. And then I was trying to open my eyes. But my eyelids seemed to be stuck for some reason. They wouldn't open. Why did they make eyelids so heavy?

At last I was able to lift them slightly. Gradually I lifted them a little more. I looked about the room and tried to focus on the shadows. My eyes closed again but I forced them to open. I felt funny — dizzy. In fact, I felt lousier than I had ever felt in my life. I tried to organize my thoughts and figure out what I was doing in a hospital, because I could tell it was a hospital. There were little bottles and gadgets attached to me. But I couldn't be here in the hospital, because I was needed somewhere. The Christmas party! Then I began remembering. I was Santa and I was riding my bicycle. Something — a car, no, a truck, a yellow truck, was coming toward me. It was becoming clear. It was lunging for me now. I moaned and blinked.

A shadow from across the room suddenly came to life and moved toward me. I saw a blurred face and then, gradually, the face acquired features. As the features cleared, I thought I recognized my sister. But Corker was in New York.

"Ben! Ben!" she said softly. "Are you waking up?" It sounded like her.

"Is that you, Corker," I tried to whisper, but my voice wasn't audible. She seemed to recognize my attempt to communicate and became excited.

"Ben! You're trying to talk, aren't you, Ben? Can you try again?" She jerked around and spoke in a whisper to another shadow. "Steve! Wake up, Steve, I think Ben is trying to say something." Steve jumped up from a chair and hurried to the side of my bed.

"Ben, old buddy?"

"Steve," I tried to say, but it sounded more like a moan. I looked back at Corker. It felt good, comforting somehow, to have them here, but I had to be tough and cool. I had to get my act together.

"What would you like to say, Ben? Is there anything you need?"

I tried to grin, but it hurt and I groaned a little. "I'm . . ."

"He said, 'I'm,' " Corker said. "Did you hear that?"

Steve nodded.

"I'm. . . . I'm . . ." I tried to smile again.

"I'm what, Ben? Go ahead. Are you hurting? What would you like to say?" Corker's voice was gentle.

"I'm . . . I'm . . . hungry." I smiled with satisfaction that I had been able to say the word.

Corker turned to Steve in amazement. "He says he's hungry. Did you hear that? He's hungry!" She began laughing and sobbing and pulling on Steve's arm. "If he's hungry, it means he's okay. He's himself!"

I watched them and smiled inside at their excitement. But then I wondered what exactly had happened, and why Corker was here, and where Mom was and how badly I was hurt. I winced as I tried to talk again. "What . . . what . . . ?"

Corker seemed to sense what I needed to know and sat down by my bed. "Ben." She tried to calm herself enough to explain. "Ben, you've been in an accident. You were badly hurt. In fact, you've already had a couple of operations, one on your ankle and one to relieve the pressure in your head. We've been so worried about you. You can't believe how worried we've been. We've been waiting for you to wake up. We thought for sure you'd wake up last night, but you didn't, and then we really started getting worried when you didn't wake up earlier today. Why do you always have to take your sweet time about everything?" She asked that with a half-laugh and a sniff.

"But thank goodness you're with us now," she went on. "Thank goodness!" She looked at Steve and added softly. "Steve administered to you, Ben. I forgot to tell you. He administered to you and . . ." Her voice cracked.

Steve sniffed too and put his arm around Corker. They hugged, smiled again, and Corker put her hand on mine. I wanted to know more and I wanted her to keep talking. I wanted to know what kind of shape I was in. "Am . . . I . . . all . . . of . . . me?"

"You're still all in one piece," Corker assured me. "You're just broken up. They're a little worried about your right ankle, but boy, we were more worried that you wouldn't come out of your coma! Thank goodness, Ben! You just don't realize how concerned we've been. Mom's been here almost constantly. Oh, my goodness! I've got to call Mom and Darlene!"

"Darlene?" I smiled a little as Corker hurried from the room. Steve put his hand on my arm.

"Your mother and Darlene have been here almost every second. We told them to go home and get some rest. Darlene has been blaming herself. She said you wouldn't have been riding that bicycle if it hadn't been for her. Do you remember the accident, Ben?"

"Yes," I said slowly. "Not . . . Darlene's . . . faul . . . t," I said. I wanted to say, "It was that idiot in the yellow truck." I was getting excited and I began to breathe heavily. "Truck! . . . I . . ."

"I know," Steve said. "Stay calm, Ben."

"He came . . . like . . . like he . . ." I wanted to tell Steve how he had lunged for me. How he had raced toward me as if he wanted to get me.

"Just relax, Ben, it's over now."

"Yes, just relax, son." It was the doctor who now smiled down at me. "I understand you're back with us," he said. "How are you feeling?"

"Not too great," I managed to slur.

"Well, under the circumstances I can understand that."

"Hav . . . ing . . . trouble . . . talk . . ."

"Your mind is working faster than your speech, and that's nothing to worry about, Ben. That will clear up soon. Now, is it all right if I ask you a few questions?"

"Sure, Doc," I slurred.

"Can you tell me your full name?" he asked.

"San . . . ta . . . Claus." I managed to stutter and I tried to smile again.

"He's just kidding," Steve assured the doctor. "He's always had trouble being serious."

Dr. Willoughby didn't smile. "Try to answer the questions straight, son."

"Ben . . . Van . . . Vleet," I said obediently.

"Good," Dr. Willoughby said. "Now can you tell me what month this is?"

"Decem . . ."

"Very good."

"And how old are you, Ben?"

"Twenty-three . . ."

"Great!"

"And . . . a . . . half," I finished. I felt as if I were taking my kindergarten entrance exam over again.

"Can you count backwards for me now, Ben?" I counted backwards.

"Fantastic, Ben! You know what, son? I think you're lucky. Not everybody who gets hit by a truck comes out of it glib of tongue, you know. And, well, frankly, you're mighty lucky to still be with us. I think that Santa suit could have had something to do with it."

I must have looked confused, because he explained. "All that padding could have protected you from the abdominal or internal injuries we usually see with this kind of an accident."

"My legs?" I asked.

"As you've probably noticed, you're in casts." He was right. I had noticed. "We're a little worried about your right ankle. There was some moderate crushing."

That was exactly the subject I wanted to talk about, and I think he could tell I was getting excited. "Doc . . . will . . . will . . . I . . . ?"

"Walk? I don't think you'll have any trouble walking again, Ben. You may limp for a while until you get —"

"Doc," I tried to raise my hand to get his attention. "Doc . . . will . . . I . . . I . . . r . . . rrrun?"

"If that ankle heals as well as we're hoping it will heal, you shouldn't have any problem putting pressure on it. It just depends on the healing, Ben." (I didn't like the sound of the word *if*, and my stomach dropped down to my back.) "Hopefully, you'll be back to normal by next summer and you won't even know you got hit by a truck. I know that's hard to believe now. Like I say, you're a lucky fellow. But right now, just be thankful you're alive and be patient."

"B . . . b . . . but . . ." I wanted him to assure me I would run. He didn't understand. I *had* to run. Running made me feel like a winner. And why had he used the word *hopefully?*

After a few more explanations, the doctor stood up to leave. "He'd better take it easy now," he said to Steve. "Let's let him rest and not talk for a while."

Corker came into the room just as the doctor said those words, and she sat down obediently in the corner away from me. Neither she nor Steve spoke.

I was glad I didn't have to talk anymore. I didn't want to talk anymore, and I didn't try to talk for quite a while. Corker finally came to my bed, looked down at me, and began straightening my covers. "Mom's coming," she whispered. "And Darlene. They should be here soon. Are you still okay?"

I didn't answer her question, but wondered instead what she was doing in Salt Lake. I managed to stutter out "New York?"

"New York went bye-bye," Corker said. I must have looked surprised, because she explained. "Lillian wasn't too delighted when I told her I had to get home fast. She fired me."

"She did?" Steve looked up, surprised. "You didn't tell me that part. You got fired just because you wanted to come see your brother? That seems a little—"

"Oh, it wasn't that. I was rude. I was upset and I said some things that I shouldn't have said. But when she suggested I take one day off and be right back I just laughed in her face, and I said, 'One day? You've got to be kidding.' I said, 'This is my brother, Lillian. Do you think your stupid fashions matter to me right now? Fashion is nothing—zero compared to my brother. What does heel height or skirt length matter to me when Ben might not make it? I couldn't care less about your show or your parties or your big-time guests. It's all terribly ridiculous right now.'

"Well, you can imagine how that went over. Lillian's life is fashion. She's devoted every minute to it. To her, it's everything. She just stared at me and said, 'I've made a serious mistake hiring you, I can see that. I thought you were committed, and now you tell me that fashion is nothing. My dear child, fashion is money, and money is everything. And to think I wanted to trust you with . . . Why you poor naive girl.' I know what she was planning to say. She was going to have me take over the business when she's gone. She thought we were exactly alike and that I was a real find. But you know what I said then, Ben? I said, 'Money is nothing, Lillian. Love, families, that's what's lasting.' Wasn't that a dumb thing to say? I mean, she isn't even a member of our church, so how could she know what that means?"

Steve was smiling gently and our eyes met. I tried to wink. "You tape-recording this?" I wanted to ask him.

I got enough out to make him understand, and he laughed. "I never have my Sony with me when I need it," he said. "But you're my witness, Ben. You heard her. I may have to remind her of that later."

Corker looked up at the ceiling and then at our faces. "Oh, you two," she said, shaking her head. Then she kind of lost control and began sobbing softly. Steve crossed the room and sat down. He put his head in his hands and looked at the floor. Then he looked up at her. I listened to her quiet sobbing and felt touched. How could I help feeling touched. My sister had just told me that I was worth more to her than Lillian's millions.

At last she stopped crying and looked up as if she were listening to something. I heard it too, a moment later. Christmas carolers were nearing, and their voices were getting louder, echoing richly down the hospital corridors. "Joy to the world, the Lord is come, Let earth receive her king . . ."

I turned my eyes toward the sound. Lights from a Christmas tree down the hall reflected in the metal on my door. "And heaven and nature sing, and heaven and nature sing . . ." The melody touched me down to my backbone and I felt a chill, but I wasn't cold.

"Ben," Corker whispered. "I guess you didn't know, did you. It's Christmas."

Christmas, I thought. *Christmas, the actual day.* And for a minute I forgot about my casts. I forgot about the fact that there was a small possibility that I might not run again. Christmas. I smiled because I could feel it again, the tingling sensation.

"Ring those Christmas bells! Ring those Christmas bells" the carolers were singing. As they passed through the hall I could see them. They were people, ordinary people, all sizes and shapes. There were little kids, teenagers, moms and dads, grand-parents. "Merry Christmas," I wanted to say to them. "Merry Christmas to you!" and I felt like giggling. I wanted to giggle because it was Christmas. I wanted to sing because the doctor was right. I was alive and lucky to be that way.

I looked at Corker and thought about what she had just told me. I looked at Steve. I thought about Mom and my aunts, my uncles, my cousins, my grandma and grandpa. I thought about all my friends, the Morgans, all the little kids in the neighbor-hood. I thought about Darlene, and love, and families. And the bells inside me started pealing. *It's Christmas, you lucky guy. You're here! You're going to be around to celebrate more Christmases. You may even be here to see your children and your grandchildren celebrate Christmases. You're alive!*

I was humming the carols to myself when I looked up and saw that Darlene had come in, wide-eyed and trembling. She reminded me of a scared little puppy, and I felt a tenderness inside. "Oh, Ben, tell me it's true! Speak to me! Can you say something?" she whispered.

I tried to smile again. "Hi ya . . . ya, kid," I said, with a slight croak.

She opened her mouth and laughed and cried at the same time. "You're here! You're here! Oh, thank goodness! It was my fault. I'm so sorry, Ben. I shouldn't have told you to take the bike, and when they called and said . . . Oh, I just about . . . Oh, Ben, please forgive me." She turned to Steve and Corker. "Has the doctor said anything about his legs. His ankle?" She started to whisper. "Will he be able to . . ."

"Let's just be happy he can think, for now," Steve said, frowning at her.

I tried to talk to her, but my voice seemed tired. I managed to be audible. "Doc says . . ." I cleared my throat.

"Please don't try to talk if you feel tired," Darlene said. "I'm sorry . . . I—"

"Doc says . . . pro . . . bably . . . if . . ."

She bit her lip, and I wanted to tell her something. I wanted to tell her that it didn't matter so much now because I was just glad to be alive—alive to see her again and my family again. I wanted to tell her that I had discovered that life is a precious gift

—the best gift I'd ever received for Christmas. But when I looked at her, her jaw was firm.

"We're going to do it, Ben. You and I are going to run a marathon next year. You just wait. You're going to make it through. Okay, Ben?"

"You and me?" I said to myself, and I smiled.

"You and me, kid," she said gently, and she leaned down and touched my cheek softly with her lips.

9

"Doing a little light reading?"

When I spoke, Corker pushed back her designer reading glasses and smiled at me. "Bon jour, sleepyhead. How are you feeling after last night?"

I chuckled and looked up at the banner still draped across the opposite wall: Hurry Back, Ben—Fastest Book Binder in the West!

"That was some New Year's Eve party, wasn't it?" I said, grinning.

"I was just afraid it would be too much for you," Corker answered. "Seventeen people in one room is a bit much. I thought that R.N. on duty would have to be taken to intensive care. She was so upset, the poor lady. She kept telling people to leave, but more just kept coming. By the way, you got some more cards and goodies this morning. Looks like the Rowler kids sent you a homemade project." She held up a picture of me looking like a combination Incredible Hulk and Egyptian mummy.

"Cute," I chuckled.

"Oh, and some more girls called and want to bring you another cake tonight. I mentioned that you've already had three cakes dropped by, but they still thought you needed theirs. It's a good thing we got you a private room."

"Under different circumstances I could really enjoy this," I said. "You know, some people don't find out how many friends they have until their funerals. Me, I was lucky." But then I added reflectively, "I'm not sure *lucky* is the right word."

"I'm not either," Corker admitted.

"Steve's blessing?"

She nodded.

"So what are we going to do about it?" I asked.

"You mean what am *I* going to do about it? You're a good Mormon. I'm the one who's been the agnostic in the family. But now I'm mixed up. I need to reanalyze a little and try to determine where I'm going from here. My little box of priorities has been badly rattled, and some things came out on top that I hadn't known were there."

"Sounds like you're in a state of flux," I said.

"Well, I just need some time to think. I need more information. Frankly, I feel as if someone has just pulled the rug out from under me."

"The rug, or your carefully laid-out goal sheet?" I asked.

She sighed. "That too. I need to make some decisions within the next little while, and that's why I'm reading this." She held up a copy of the Book of Mormon. "I just can't stand not knowing what I'm doing."

I grunted when I noticed that she was well into the book — the book I had never even opened. I looked up at the blank television screen while Corker went back to her reading. If football wasn't on already it would be on soon, and it was Super Bowl day. All I needed to do was push a little button, and if that was too much trouble, Corker or a nurse would do it for me. But I just kept staring at the blank screen instead, because I knew Corker was wrong about something.

She was wrong about my being a good Mormon. I wasn't. I was a half-Mormon, if there is such a thing. Sure, I went to my meetings, obeyed the "Thou shalt nots," and even lived the Word of Wisdom, but I wasn't a whole Latter-day Saint. I was a "go-to-church-but-don't-let-it-get-to-you" type of Mormon. My spiritual mind was about as blank as the television screen above me.

I had more or less motivated myself to become physically fit.

Some people are self-motivated to spiritual fitness, but not me. Me, I had to walk down death's corridor to recognize the fact that I was a spiritual weakling.

After I had stared at the screen for a while, I looked back at Corker. "Feel like reading out loud?" I asked her.

"Sure," she said. "I'll start over." She flipped back to the beginning of the book, pulled her chair closer, and began reading First Nephi, chapter one.

" 'I, Nephi, having been born of goodly parents, therefore I was taught somewhat in all the learning of my father; and having seen many afflictions in the course of my days, nevertheless . . .' " I was beginning to relate to Nephi already. When Corker came to the part that said he was "large of stature," I liked this Nephi even more.

Corker was just starting chapter seven when Steve walked in.

"Ah, music to my ears," he said.

Corker smiled up at him. "Hi," she said softly, taking off her glasses. He put his hand gently on her shoulder for a moment and then thumped me on the chest lightly.

"How's it going today, Big Ben?"

"They're calling me a miracle," I answered. "Dr. Willoughby says my rapid speed of recovery is remarkable."

"Good news! Maybe you'll be able to go home soon, if you keep up the good work."

"I'd say it was *your* good work, pal."

He shook his head but didn't comment, because he was looking at Corker and the Book of Mormon in her hand. "I was thinking maybe we could get a little study group going after you're home, Ben," he said, still looking at Corker. "Darlene said she'd be interested too. I could pull out the old missionary discussions and we could talk about them or we could just try to answer any questions anybody might have. I need to get back to my scripture study too."

"Why wait?" I said. "Let's start today. How about right after dinner."

"Sounds fine with me. Sound all right with you, Corker?" he asked cautiously.

"Sure, I'll go along with that. I do have a few questions." Steve's eyes met mine for just an instant before he looked back at Corker thoughtfully.

Later that day, and for the next few evenings, Corker, Steve, Darlene, and I talked about the gospel. Corker had questions all right! Her questions were difficult, probing, often challenging. As the discussions continued, her questions became even more difficult, probing, challenging — and argumentative. By using his spiritual sensitivity, scriptural backup, and good old reasoning power, Steve came up with answers. But Corker never seemed satisfied. She kept shooting back with more questions. We couldn't seem to get the discussion off the ground, and something felt wrong. Steve figured out what was going on before I could put my finger on it.

"You know, Corker, this isn't a game of Ping-Pong," he said.

"Chess?" she asked sheepishly, as though she knew she had just been found out.

"No," Steve said rather sternly. "It isn't any kind of a contest. I'm not sure why you're competing, but I don't think I want to be a part of it."

"Why, because I have some difficult questions — questions that maybe you don't have the answers to?"

"No, because I don't think you really want to hear any answers. You're too busy thinking up new questions."

Corker knew it was true, and her face pinkened.

Steve changed his tactics. "Are you praying about this, Corker?" he asked quietly and gently, as he looked into her eyes.

"Of course." She answered without meeting his eyes. "I try to have a prayer in my heart. I don't get down on my knees or anything, if that's what you mean."

"Maybe you should."

That made Corker angry. "What's that supposed to mean?"

"Just what it says — maybe you should. It might make a difference."

"It doesn't matter how you pray as long as you pray," Corker argued. "Look at Ben. He can't get down on his knees. Does that mean his prayers aren't heard?"

"Sometimes the physical is a forerunner of the spiritual," Steve said. "And kneeling is symbolical."

"Of what?"

"What do you think?"

We all knew Corker was smart enough to figure out what kneeling symbolized. Finally she said it. "Humility, I suppose."

Then she surprised us all. "I guess that *is* something I could use a little more of."

Amen to that, I thought.

"Don't say it, Ben," she said, without looking at me.

"I wouldn't dream of it," I answered, wondering how she had read my mind.

"Why don't you give it a try tonight," Steve suggested. "Kneel by your bed—"

"Don't push me, Steve."

Steve sighed. "No one is trying to push you, Corker. Don't you see, it's entirely up to you. No one can ever force you to accept the gospel, or even to learn about it with an open mind, for that matter. If you don't want to, there isn't anything any of us can do about it. It's entirely up to you. You're a free agent."

Corker seemed to like that, and she was quiet for a few moments. Finally she spoke. "I guess it couldn't hurt to try."

Nothing more was ever said about kneeling, but during the next study groups Corker seemed to be listening more, talking less. She still asked questions, but this time she wanted the answers. The spirit in our meetings became calmer, and we all began climbing rungs together. Pretty soon, Corker was gaining momentum and speed-climbing. In a matter of days we could sense the spiritual enthusiasm exploding inside of her.

As far as I was concerned, spiritual fitness seemed easier to acquire than I had expected it to be. The bishop had loaned me a set of scripture tapes, and all I needed to do was push a button and lie back and listen. At first I thought push-button spiritual fitness was a pretty great way to go.

But when I listened to a tape of the New Testament that told me about a man named Jesus, I determined that spiritual fitness was much more than I had thought it was. I realized that his life exemplified true courage, a different kind of courage than I had always tried to have. His courage made him do what was right no matter what it took, and it wasn't the "make yourself look good" kind of courage. He maintained that courage even when some of his buddies turned on him. One even turned him in. But he followed through with what he had to do. And there was more about him that I couldn't understand. It was the unselfishness. I puzzled over his motivation. I found myself thinking about him more and more, and about what he had done for all of us—for me. I knew then that becoming spiritually fit wasn't going to be as simple as it had looked at first. It meant I would have to change myself.

I was listening to Mark, chapter eight, when I looked up and noticed that a guy was standing in my doorway. He was a big kid, maybe nineteen or twenty, and he wasn't leaning against the door frame, he was just standing there in the middle looking awkward and ill-at-ease. I didn't know him, but then, I had had other visitors I didn't know.

"Hi," I said. "Looking for someone?"

"Are you Ben Van Vleet?" he asked.

"In person," I answered. "What can I do for you?" I clicked off my recorder.

He slouched in slowly, and I could see he was shaking.

"You okay?" he asked.

Are you *okay?* I thought, because his voice was quaking so hard I could hardly understand him. Then I said, "Oh, you know. Under the circumstances I'm not too bad, considering I was hit by a truck." My eyes were turned toward him, mainly because it was difficult to turn the rest of me.

At the word *truck* he winced slightly and his face paled. "Do I know you?" I asked. I was becoming suspicious. The fact that he couldn't seem to look me in the eye bothered me. He just kept looking at my casts and my mummylike appearance. Finally he looked at the floor and started pushing at something with his foot.

"Hey, am I supposed to know you?" I repeated hopefully.

He shook his head and then he changed his mind and he nodded, lowering himself into a chair. "I drive a yellow truck," he said quietly.

"Oh!" My suspicions were confirmed. I clenched my fist. I wanted to cream this guy, this guy who had nearly done me in and now had the gall to come into my room and sit on my chair. But I could hardly cream him in my present state, so I just lay there churning inside. When I spoke, I spoke bitterly.

"It's so nice of you to stop by," I said. "How wonderful of you to check on me after nearly doing me in. Where's your truck, by the way. I sure hope I didn't dent your fender."

"I'm just glad you made it," he whispered, ignoring my sarcasm. "Man, I'm just glad you're still—"

"Well, now, so am I." I was trembling now, and my words were spurting out. "Hey, I've been hoping you'd stop by because I've been wanting to ask you something. Tell me, was it anything personal? Did I get in front of you in a line once? I mean, you lunged for me like you had my number. It was no accident. You deliberately—"

"I know."

"You know. You admit it then?"

He nodded and looked down at his feet. His lip twitched, and finally he stared into my glaring eyes. "It wasn't you I was after. It didn't have anything to do with you. I wanted to wipe out Santa Claus."

"Oh, I see. Yes, that makes a lot of sense. Why? Why, were you a bad boy this year, or something?"

He nodded again. "I think I've got it all figured out. I think I know now. It took me a while to figure it out, but it's this way. When you're doing okay and you feel good about yourself, then you feel good about other people and about life. But, I was feeling lousy about myself."

"Oh, well, isn't that too bad?" I started to say. "Isn't it too bad for me that—"

"It started happening a few years ago. Some buddies and I started goofing off. We'd do crazy things—really crazy things—and we thought we were clever. Then I started boozing and taking stuff with these same guys and we *really* thought we were clever. But now I don't feel so clever."

He paused and seemed to sigh before going on. "Anyway, I'd been drinking when I saw you, I mean Santa, and I remembered that my parents had just kicked me out this Christmas and that it would be a lousy Christmas and I wanted to . . ." He lowered his head and shook it. "I can't believe that I really wanted to wipe him out. I really hated him. I hated Santa Claus." He turned his head away from me and ran the back of his hand across his eyes.

Something he had said must have hit a nerve in me, because I was listening. I tried to back up and remember what it was he had said. What was it that had made me start listening? "Run that by me again," I said.

"What?"

"What you said before the part about your boozing."

He looked up. "Just that my buddies and I did some crazy things just for laughs."

"Things that didn't make any sense?"

"Right! We'd go out late at night and stir up trouble."

"And that was before you started the heavier stuff?"

"Right."

I must have been staring at him—at his flushed face and blurry eyes; and I kept staring at his face—the face I had wanted to smash my fist into. This was the guy I had wanted to cream. This was the guy I had hated. But I couldn't hate him now. How could I when I was looking at myself? It came to me that he was like the guy I might have been if it hadn't been for the Morgans and for the Church. I knew it could have been me in his shoes. And I had the suspicion that if I could choose between his shoes and my casts, I wouldn't take the shoes. I kept staring at him and my clenched fist loosened.

"Anyway," he said. "I . . . I came to tell you that . . . that for what it's worth, I'm sorry. I know that doesn't do you a whole lot of good right now, but I'm sorry. Man, I don't know if I could have lived with myself if you'd . . . I'm just glad you . . . You don't know how glad I am that you're . . ."

I felt strange inside. I wasn't angry anymore. I wasn't anything. I just knew I couldn't judge this guy—the guy who could have been me. Then gradually, as I stared at him, at his hollow-eyed paleness, a warmth enveloped me. Call it empathy, call it love, I'm not sure what it was, but it was there just because he was there and because . . . yes, because he was my brother.

"Hey, buddy." I interrupted him, and he stopped talking. "It took guts for you to come here. Thanks." He looked into my eyes to see if I meant the words. I smiled slightly. "And you ought to be mighty glad about something."

"What's that?"

"You ought to be mighty glad I wasn't the real Santa."

"The real Santa?" he asked numbly.

"Boy, would you have been in trouble if I'd been the real Santa. You would have had a zillion little kids out there ready to cream you. You wouldn't have been able to show your face anywhere."

His mouth pulled up a little at the corner and he chuckled a little nervously. "Yes, I hadn't thought of that. I guess that's right."

I touched his arm, because I knew there was something else he was hoping to hear. The words flowed from me without mental strain. "I can't condemn you or judge you, because I'd be condemning myself. I mean, I've just been reading about Christ, the man who took all our sins on himself and then asked forgiveness for those who crucified him. Besides, I've been where you were. At least, I would have been there if . . . well, the Mormon Church and some neighbors, Mormon neighbors, saved my life."

He grunted, and I could sense his rebelliousness and bitterness. "I'm not a Mormon. I used to be but . . . I can't stand the . . . the—"

"Preaching. The 'be good' sermons. I know. Like I say, I was there." I paused. "How about doing me a favor? It's important."

"Anything. You name it," he said.

I picked up a copy of the Book of Mormon. "I want you to read this book."

"The Book of Mormon?"

"I know. I know. That's the last thing you want to read. But you owe me one."

"I know, but—"

"No buts. I want you to read this book because it's cool. It's not what you think it is. It's . . . it's right." He took the book from me slowly. "Now go out there and clean up your act." I paused and grinned. "Because if you don't I'm going to find you. And maybe I'll buy myself a yellow truck. Hey, what's your name. I don't even know your name."

"Scott . . . Scott Burroughs."

"Yeah, well Scott Burroughs, I mean it, okay?"

"Okay. I guess the first thing I need to do is turn myself in because . . . I . . . And I guess I could read this."

"Promise me you will."

"Okay, I'll read it."

"And let me know," I added. "Let me know what happens to you, Scott, because . . . because I care." It felt good to say the words.

"Thanks." That seemed to get to him. His lip trembled for a second and then he was gone.

I looked at the doorway for quite a while, and then I turned my eyes toward the window and looked at the sky. I was filled with an elation. It had begun raining outside, and suddenly I loved the rain. Suddenly I loved the rain and the sky and the people . . . all the people in the hospital, and I wanted to hug them all. I loved my friends who had sent me things, and I loved the people who hadn't. I even loved the people I didn't know, the people I had never met. And all because I loved Scott Burroughs, the guy who had hit me in his yellow truck.

It wasn't long till Corker came rushing into the room. Before I had a chance to tell her about what had just happened, she began waving a letter at me. "You'll never believe this. I got a letter from Lillian. Listen to this:

> You are a gritty child. The more I thought about what you had the nerve to say to me, the angrier I became. I became furious, and I stayed that way for days. As you know, my whole life has been fashion. I couldn't understand why I was so angry until I realized that what you said was the truth. Thoreau said something similar in *Walden*.
>
> I will always love fashion, but what you said about families struck me. (Corker looked up and smiled at this point. "Wait till you hear this.") You said "Families are forever." I had a family once, but I had put them out of my mind. You see, my mother and father were killed during the war. Then, what you said about families made me stop to think. How do I know they are not still alive and waiting for me somewhere in a heavenly place. The more I thought about that the more excited I became. I have a niece and two nephews somewhere and I'm going to look for them. I never cared before but now I want to find them.
>
> And I think your statement dug even deeper. I started thinking about love. I've been like Scrooge, always seeking more money. I wasn't happy with a mere million. I wanted two and then three, but I hoarded it and didn't share it. This Christmas I began thinking about that, and I realized it was because I wasn't at peace with myself. I wasn't able to face

my own pain and hatred so that I could wipe it out of my life.

I have never revealed my soul like this, especially in a letter, but I thought it might be important to tell you that I have donated over $100,000 to the poor this Christmas. It was delightful doing it. And it's all because I began thinking about families. We are, after all, one big family, aren't we?

Corker, if your brother is recovering well, I would like to ask you to return when you can and work for me once again. Maybe you can help me remember.

"So," Corker said quickly, "I've got to mail her a copy of the Book of Mormon right away and tell her that I love her and that she's like family to me and tell her about sealings and send the missionaries. And there are also some other copies I've got to get sent."

I had been wondering why she had her portable typewriter and a roll of labels. "You mean like some Congressmen and movie stars and a prime minister or two?"

"I've listed forty-two names in all. I knew there was a reason I kept a copy of all their addresses on three-by-five cards."

I smiled, shook my head, and rolled my eyeballs. Then I asked cautiously, "What about her offer? Are you going to go back to New York?"

"Of course not. I can't." She mumbled, as she searched for something in her purse.

"Well, I'm relieved to hear that."

"You know very well I'm going to stay here and marry Steve." She was smiling softly as she put a pencil in her mouth and continued looking through her purse.

"Does he know yet?"

"Of course," she mumbled. "He just hasn't asked me officially yet, but he will."

I couldn't argue with her assumption. "Yes, I suppose he will, at that." I wanted to know how she felt now about children, but I didn't ask her. "And you feel good about it now, huh?" I said instead.

"Ben, I *know* the Church is true. I didn't want it to be true, but it is. And the Mormon Church means families, and families means Steve and me. And that's the way it should be and that's the way it's going to be, and to tell you the truth, I've never been happier." She hesitated for just a moment, and I knew why she was hesitating. "I'm not saying I know all the answers or how this is going to turn out, but I just know it's the right thing."

She got out her labels and set up her typewriter.

"You're going to type labels now?"

"Yes," she answered matter-of-factly. But she looked up suddenly. "Ben, I forgot to mention one thing."

"What's that?"

"I love him. I've always loved him."

"I already knew that," I said. Corker smiled, put the pencil over her ear and began typing madly.

I looked back out of the window at the sky and felt a strange peacefulness. It didn't matter that Corker was sending out forty-two copies of the Book of Mormon. It didn't matter that she was running circles around me again. It didn't matter at all.

10

"We have something important to tell you." Corker and Steve were holding hands and smiling smugly.

"Hmmm, let me think. What could it be? Should I act surprised?"

"I guess not," Steve said, sounding a little disappointed. "Unless you want to fake it."

"Are you sure you two have known each other long enough?" I grinned around the carrot stick in my mouth.

He ignored my question and asked one of his own. "How about being my best man?"

I stopped chewing the carrot stick and swallowed hard. "You bet I would!"

"Do you think you'll feel well enough by March the fourth?" he asked, looking at my still swollen hand and my legs.

"You can count on it," I said quickly. I nodded. "You can count on it!" Then I nodded again. "March the fourth, huh? That's appropriate for you two. March the fourth! It makes a statement. Corker and Steve are marching forth on March the fourth!"

But it was just a week after their announcement that Corker received a letter from New York which made her gasp slightly. Her eyes grew large, and they remained that way as she looked over the letter at me. She folded it carefully and put it back into the envelope. I decided not to ask her any questions or pry for information until she was ready. Later, as she was sitting at the kitchen table staring at the calendar, she looked up at me and bit her lip.

"What's up?" I asked. "Something's sure been gnawing at you today."

"Lillian wrote," she said, tapping her pencil.

"And what did the little lady have to say?"

"She offered me a raise—a very substantial raise. I don't even know if I'm worth it."

"Now that must be *some raise*," I kidded.

She remained serious, but her eyes grew large again. "It *is*! Believe me!" She blew out a sigh. "It *is*. I've just been sitting here thinking, Ben—if I went back East for just a few short months, I could earn a lot of money for Steve and me. I could earn enough for Steve's schooling, or maybe a down payment on a house or duplex or something. Maybe more than just a down payment. We could practically . . . well . . . it's tempting."

"You mean postpone your wedding?"

"Possibly . . . just for a few months. Or . . . or we could go ahead and get married, if I could talk Steve into going to Columbia University for a while—just a year or two—and we could postpone having our family for just that long, maybe even less time, just a very short while . . . But I don't know if Steve would go for it. I think I'll mention it to him tonight."

I wanted to start preaching to her, but I decided against it. "I guess that's something you'll have to figure out," I said, and she looked up, surprised. But then I couldn't help myself, and I added, "Money isn't—"

"Money isn't everything," she repeated in a nasal tone.

The next morning I was eager to hear what had happened, and I asked Corker at breakfast. "What did Steve say about your proposal?"

She smiled a small smile. "I guess Steve knows how to handle me these days."

I grinned. "Really put his foot down, huh? Told you 'no' in no uncertain terms and let you know who was boss?"

"Come on, Ben!" She puckered her lips in disgust. "I *said* he knows how to handle me. If he had said 'Absolutely not,' I probably would have wanted to go very, very badly and I probably would have *gone*—maybe. At least, I would have resented him for the rest of our lives. You know I just can't stand people to tell me I can't do something. I just hate that. But Steve is no dummy."

"So what did he say?" I asked.

"We . . . e . . . ell," she smiled. "He suggested I pray about it."

"Oh, I see." I nodded. "You're right. Steve is no dummy. And? Did you?"

"Yes, I did," she sighed. "But sometimes you know the answer to a prayer before you even pray it. Darn!" She pursed her lips again. "I did kind of want to be rich and big time for a while longer. Oh, well!"

It wasn't easy to hide my amusement.

The frenzy of the wedding preparations actually made me forget that I was getting older every day and that my twenty-fourth birthday was on the countdown. My birthday comes every year on the same day: February 10. Every year, Mom had remembered it. But on this particular February 10 she was into the heavy wedding preparations. I'd never seen her so giddy one minute and so gloomy the next. For someone who had been planning this wedding for years, Mom still seemed to have plenty to get flustered over.

Corker, luckily, was quite mellow about letting Mom have her way often. I was the go-between, and whenever there was a real difference of opinion, they asked my opinion. That's a dangerous position to find yourself in. Luckily, there weren't many differences of opinion.

On my birthday, I was addressing envelopes for the invitations at our kitchen table until Corker saw my handwriting. "Good grief," she said. "They'll think we took these to the zoo for the chimpanzees to address. And you're getting grease spots all over them. Ben, for heaven's sakes!" She grabbed the envelopes away from me.

"For rude," I shot back. "I can't help it if I'm not left-handed." Then I couldn't resist: "I thought people were supposed to be nice to you on your birthday."

We had just eaten dinner, and I had really expected Mom to bring out a birthday cake for dessert, but she hadn't. Now she was clearing the table. At my words she stopped dead still. Her mouth dropped open and her face lost its color. I felt rotten for having mentioned my birthday.

"Oh, no!" she gasped. "Oh, no! I can't believe I forgot. Ben, I really did it, honey. To think we almost didn't have you for this birthday, and then I forgot." She jumped up and started throwing open cupboards—looking for a cake mix, I presumed.

"Hey, Mom, don't. It doesn't matter," I half-laughed.

"Of course it does," she said. "It matters a great deal. Oh, I can't believe it." She had found a cake mix and was pouring it into the mixing bowl when the doorbell rang.

"Anybody home?" Darlene, Frances, Bishop Morgan, and Steve were standing on the porch. Frances was holding a huge cake with "Happy Birthday to the Toughest Kid in the West" on it. Two cowboys on it were having a gun fight. Darlene was hiding something behind her back. I chuckled excitedly.

"You saved the day!" Mom sounded relieved and exuberant. "You saved the day, you adorable people!"

"They always do," I added quietly.

"Ta-da!" Darlene pulled out a big box wrapped in cowboy wrapping paper. I ripped off the paper eagerly but remembered to say "For me?" when I was already down to the box. Darlene giggled happily as I pulled out a pair of jogging shoes. The "in" kind that all the high school kids just *had* to wear.

"Wow!" I said. "These things cost a fortune."

"Well, they're from everybody. And this is from me," she said, handing me another, smaller package.

"More?" I began tearing eagerly again. Inside I found a mint green jogging suit.

"Nice," I said.

"Well, no offense, but your old suit made you look like Big Bird."

"I know," I agreed. "Hey, thanks. This is terrific stuff. Maybe I'll wear it to the doctor's office tomorrow and see if I can inspire them to take off my casts."

"You're going tomorrow, huh?" Darlene said. "Well, good luck." She held up crossed fingers. Suddenly I noticed she was wearing a suit the same color as the one in the box.

"Hey!" I pointed to her suit. "Hey!" I pointed to the box. "All right! We'll match!" But then some other recent thoughts returned, and my exuberance faded.

If things had been hectic before the invitations were out, they were hysterical afterwards. I was happy that I had two arms and a leg to use now, however, so that I could help a little. All I had left from my "mummy" look was a walking cast. I had enough mobility now to answer the door when nobody else was available and let the delivery man unload the gifts in our entry. Hundreds of gifts had poured in already from neighbors, old friends, ward members, and there were quite a few from back East and even some from foreign countries — from important people who had fallen in love with Corker during her short time in New York.

Then a gift arrived which was disguised as a letter. When Corker opened it, her eyes grew large. "Oh, my!" She went right to the phone and dialed Steve's number. "You'll never believe this! Guess what Lillian sent us! Two round-trip tickets to France, and listen to this: A honeymoon on the French Riviera, all expenses paid! I can't believe it! I can't believe it!" she started repeating. I couldn't believe it either.

"It sure beats Lava Hot Springs," I said when she was off the phone.

"Oh, my!" Corker repeated again. But within seconds she jumped up and was back on the wedding preparation job.

I've often wondered why two people can't just get married, why they have to have flowers, special clothes, refreshments, photographs taken, and thousands of worries. Why does getting married have to be such a complex affair? I guess civilized life just isn't simple. Corker's gown, which was being shipped from back East, finally arrived just four days before the wedding. Even I had to admit it was pretty nice. It looked like Corker: sleek and elegant. It also looked expensive. *And* it looked like the kind of a dress a fashion expert would pick out. So did the bridesmaids' dresses, for that matter. They were light and airy and the kind of dresses that make girls look like girls. *Feminine,* is the word, I guess. Corker had chosen blue and coral colors, and that seemed to be important because everything had to go with those two colors, even the cake.

If my fingers had cooperated we could have had the cake done early, but we had to save the frosting part until the last minute. There wasn't a lot of decorating to do, because of the fresh flowers. A florist would help us pick out flowers and arrange them. It looked like everything was go and we started the countdown: Ten days . . . seven days . . . four days . . . three . . . two . . . one day. And then it was March the fourth.

If someone had told me six months before that Corker, the woman of steel, and "Big Ben," the toughest guy in the West, would be dressed in white, waiting in a room that looked heavenly, to have some important and eternal sealing work done, some heavenly business taken care of, I wouldn't have believed them.

Corker passed by me on Steve's arm and she reached out for my hand and squeezed it. Mom was trying to hold me up, or I was trying to hold her up, I'm not sure which. "Corker's always wondered what heaven looks like," Mom whispered in my ear. "When she was little she took Daddy's shaving—"

"I know, I remember," I said. "Well, now she knows. This place *looks* like heaven, doesn't it."

We lowered ourselves to the velvet chairs and watched as Steve and Corker kneelèd across from each other at the altar. Mom sighed and sniffed, and I held my breath. It was quite an experience to see my best buddy and my baby sister look into each other's eyes and make their eternal vows. In fact, when I let myself breathe, I got a little choked up. But then I saw my face in the mirrors that reflected into each other, symbolizing eternity, and I forced myself to cool it. All I needed was to see myself (and have others see me) whimpering into eternity.

It was our turn next and I kneeled with Corker and Mom at the altar. Bishop Morgan stepped in to take Dad's place. It was quite a moment when we were joined together for eternity as a family unit. Steve helped Corker up and took her in his arms, and then we were all hugging each other.

What a day it was! Of course there were pictures to be taken on the grounds of the temple, and there wasn't much time to spare before the wedding breakfast. That's why I couldn't figure out why Mom had wandered to a corner of the waiting room. Finally she bustled over to me. "Why on earth were you talking to yourself in the corner," I asked.

"I wasn't talking to myself," she said. "I was promising your dad that I wouldn't nag him! Not ever again—not for the rest of eternity!" She smiled sweetly as she started crying again. "Ben, I think this has been the most beautiful day of my life."

"Me too," I admitted quietly. "Me too, Mom. And there's more to come. Think you can take it?"

"I sure can! Let's go!"

The reception that evening was one of those receptions that girls probably dream about. No one knew about the last-minute problems, such as the photographer forgetting his film and Frances's zipper breaking. Otherwise, it was almost as if Mom had been planning this thing for years. Maybe because she had. The gifts, of course, were out of this world. But then, so was everything. People oo-ed and ah-ed over the dresses, the flowers, the refreshments, the table decorations (bowls of blue water with daisies floating in them) and, of course, the elegant cake. Corker looked radiant as she charmed the guests who came through the wedding line. She hugged a lot of people and looked into their eyes with tears in her own, as if the steel had melted and was bubbling over. Steve clasped their hands and patted their backs. Naturally, I joked with everyone who came through. But I also kept staring at Darlene, because I wasn't used to seeing her dressed like that. She was usually sporty or tailored, and she always looked good. But in that bridesmaid's dress she was absolutely stunning.

Well, the big days in our lives go by just as quickly and have the same number of hours in them as other days. Soon the cake was cut, the rice had been thrown, and it was all over. And Corker and Steve were off into eternity with a rattle of tin cans.

Darlene was jabbering about the wedding as she drove us home, but I was quiet. The oldies but goodies radio station was playing a song from *Camelot,* and the lyrics struck me as ironical. "If ever I would leave you, it wouldn't be in springtime. . . ." Darlene finished raving about the reception and started chattering about the Twenty-fourth of July marathon coming up.

"Maybe that would be a little soon for your ankle. Maybe we should aim for the St. George marathon at the end of the summer." She was enthusiastic because the doctor seemed to think my ankle was healing even better than he had dared to hope.

"Darlene." I interrupted her just as we pulled into the driveway, and she stopped talking as if she could sense by my voice that I had something important to say. "Darlene, I have something to tell you."

"Okay," she said quietly. "What is it?"

I yawned, tapped at the dash board, stretched my eyes. She turned off the engine. "Well, it's just that I don't think I'll be running in a marathon this year or the next."

She looked puzzled. "But I thought the doctor said your ankle —"

"It's not because of my ankle. It's something else. It's . . . uh . . ." It was even harder to tell her than I had thought it would be. I bit my bottom lip and flipped it out as I noticed how her face glowed.

"What? Go ahead, Ben."

"Okay," I said, feeling funny inside. "It looks like I'm going to be doing something else next year and the year after, and —"

"What?" she said. "What are you getting at?"

I sighed. "I've been doing some serious thinking about this, and some . . . well, some serious praying, and I've already talked to the bishop about it, and —"

"You're going on a mission?" Her eyes grew large.

"Right!" I paused and then continued. "Now, I know what you're thinking. You're thinking, 'But, Big Ben, you're twenty-four years old. You're an old man. You'll be twenty-six when you come home. Now that's *really* old.' You're probably thinking that to yourself."

I didn't let her respond. "But my question, Darlene, is this: Just how old would I be if I didn't go on a mission — twenty-six, right? Had you thought of that? Huh? Because —"

Darlene put her hand over my mouth. "Ben," she said quietly. "I wasn't thinking that at all."

"You weren't?"

She shook her head. "I was just thinking what a super missionary you're going to be." She shook her head again. "Wow! Somebody like you — a people lover. Think of all the good you could do. You're a winner, Ben!"

"I know," I said. "I mean . . ."

"I know what you mean." She smiled and the moonlight reflected in her glimmering eyes. "I know what you mean," she repeated.

11

After she had had a fairy-tale wedding and a honeymoon at what the brochures call the "French Paradise," I was afraid Corker's advent into domesticity would be quite a letdown. I wondered how she would handle her role of wife and home-maker.

Knowing the Corker, I was sure she would eventually conquer the skills and reign supreme as a queen in her kitchen and her home, but the learning process can be painful in areas where talent is scanty. To be fair, though, Corker wasn't neces-sarily untalented in domestic pursuits. Let's be kind and say she had an experience void. I also didn't know if she would be able to admit she was bottom rung.

Anyway, Corker plunged into homemaking and cooking with a series of marathons. Because she liked to stick to some-thing until she was good at it, she made Jell-O until she had the process down. She experimented with different flavors and fruits, until on the twelfth day she and Steve came over for their weekly visit. "I plan to move on to cookies next," Corker announced.

"Right away?" Steve asked eagerly.

I could have sworn good humor filtered through her eyes when she said, "Steve told me he's turning into a 'Jell-O belly.'"

Steve smiled. "I think Corker makes the best Jell-O I've ever tasted. Her lemon Jell-O with whipping cream and banana and pineapple is tops, but it's been almost two weeks of Jell-O, and I'm beginning to jiggle inside when I walk. I feel like I'm becoming soft-set." Corker laughed, and I tried to remember if I had ever heard her laughing at herself.

"I've already made chocolate chip cookies," she said.

"And they were terrific," Steve added. "Just one or two tasted a little salty. The others — wow!"

"That reminds me," Corker said. "Where does Mom keep that cookie recipe book. You know, the one with the picture of kids eating cookies on it."

"It's in the far cabinet on the sink side," I answered.

While Corker was out of the room, Steve whispered to me, "Ben, next time you give Corker a recipe, would you mind writing the words *tablespoon* and *teaspoon* out for her? I don't think she understands the difference in the abbreviations, and she gets them mixed up."

I chuckled. "I hope you live through this, Steve."

"Hey, no problem! I can live through anything with my Corker. She's really doing great. It's just one or two details like the salt, for instance. And we've discussed the art of not mixing colors in the laundry and reading labels carefully. She complained that my woolen socks didn't have labels, and she had a point."

"You're a good man," I said.

"She's a great gal, Ben. She's independent, though. She doesn't want me to help her. She says she wants to prove to herself that she can do it alone, first. You know the Corker."

I nodded.

"Ben, I'm crazy about her," Steve added. "I'm looney about her, as you put it. I really love her."

"That's nice to hear," I said. "I think it should be a policy that people love each other when they get married."

Corker must have heard the last words he spoke, because when she came into the room, carrying three cookbooks, she blew Steve a kiss, and she glowed for the rest of the visit.

I lost track of Corker's marathons after that, since I was busy making preparations of my own. I was doing some exercises of the old muscles again to try to get back into shape for tracting, and I was still working vigorously on my spiritual intellect. The void was gradually filling up. I had put in my papers and it looked as if I would soon be heading for the MTC and then for some remote part of the world. I wondered where.

Mom, who had barely started living a normal life and had finally adjusted herself to life without Corker, was off and running again, this time on preparations for my farewell and the open house. Again she was giddy one minute and gloomy the next. She took the last of her vacation off to clean house, shop, and so on, but she wasted almost one entire day crying because I had received my mission call. I had opened the envelope ready for any remote area and hoping the natives would not be too wild and restless. The call was to Southern California.

Now Mom was up on a ladder washing ceilings and walls, even though I had tried to convince her that nobody at the open house would examine our ceilings and walls.

"Ben," she said. "Hand me that yellow cloth, would you? No, I mean the blue one. Now hand me a hanky."

"One hanky coming up." I noticed she was whimpering again.

"I just can't believe how quickly you two have grown, and now you'll both be gone from me. I know that's selfish of me, but, oh, Ben, my two babies will be gone and—"

"Mom, I'm twenty-four years old. Wouldn't you say it's about time?"

"Yes, I suppose so, but I still can't believe it. Well, I'm not going to cry anymore, and that's that. There's just too much to do." She handed back the hanky. "I should have been better prepared for this. I should have been ready months ago."

"Months ago? You didn't *know* months ago."

"Of course I knew. I've known you would go on a mission for years."

"Come again? How could you know I would go on a mission when I didn't know myself."

"Ben," Mom said patiently, "a mother just knows things. Now, you have always taken your sweet time about things, but you've always come through. Sometimes you're just a little slower getting there than you should be and sometimes you just need a little better reason than others do, but you always pull through."

I was happy in my mother's confidence in my dependability,

but the next thing she said threw me for a loop. "For years I've been preparing what I'd say in my talk at your farewell."

"For years? What have you been writing down?"

"Just the pranks you've pulled. The only thing that kept me going sometimes was the knowledge that someday I could get even with you and share with everyone at your farewell all the awful things you've done."

I must have looked a little surprised, because she started giggling. "Yes, I've kept track of every prank you've ever played."

"Well, that's wonderful to hear," I said. "Yes, that's real wonderful to hear." I was feeling very insecure.

Mom climbed down from the ladder, and I followed her into the kitchen. "Like what kinds of things?"

"You'll find out," she said mysteriously.

"Hey, there isn't anything written that says mothers have to tell all at farewells, you know. In fact, maybe I won't even ask you to speak."

"You've got to," she said. "I've already told several people that I'm going to tell about your pranks, and they're coming just to hear about them."

"Nice of them," I mumbled. Mom was smirking and seemed to be enjoying herself immensely.

"You're just kidding," I said. "I can tell."

Two weeks later, I wondered. The chapel was packed and the cultural hall was fairly full. I kept wondering if these were a few of the people Mom had told. People like to hear about jokes and pranks. That's why they always turn to "Life in These United States" first when they pick up a *Reader's Digest.*

But I stopped worrying about what Mom planned to tell as it got closer to starting time for sacrament meeting. I had something else to worry about. Corker and Steve were scheduled to give the prayers, and they hadn't arrived yet. They had flown to New York for a few days at Lillian's invitation. Lillian was as crazy about Steve as she was about Corker, and she had said she wanted "her kids" to have a little R and R between quarters and at the same time see a sneak preview of her upcoming line at an exclusive little party for her best friends. She had also mentioned some religious questions. Corker and Steve had planned to fly home late Saturday, take a cab from the airport, and have all night to rest up for my farewell. I had teased them about being jet setters.

I looked at the organist and hoped she would play the prelude music a few minutes longer than usual. My eyes kept shifting from her to the rear door of the chapel and then back again to the organist. When I looked at Mom, she was playing the same anxious game as I was. During the opening song we both were still looking yearningly at the back door, till finally we exchanged glances and both sighed visibly. At that point Corker and Steve entered and came rushing up the aisle. Corker looked like a fashion plate in a chic suit, and Steve, who always looked cool even when he was rushing, looked . . . well, cool.

"They're on the last verse of the opening song," I whispered to Corker when she and Steve sat down next to me in the seats we had reserved. "That's what I call cutting it close."

"We didn't think we were going to make it," she whispered. "We missed a flight in Chicago and we were stuck in the airport for hours. We just barely drove in from the Salt Lake airport. We had to change in the restroom here." The last verse ended, and she bounced up to give the opening prayer.

Even though she was still a little out of breath, Corker offered a simple yet classy prayer. I guess it seemed beautiful to me because it was sincere. Towards the end, she said, "Please help Ben to know how much we love him, how much we care about him. Help him to know that we are confident in him, and that we know he'll be an outstanding missionary and servant for thee." For a moment I wondered how Corker had learned to pray so eloquently in the short period of her Church activity, but naturally she'd learn that fast too, once she set her mind to it.

When it was Mom's turn to speak, she turned to smile at me just before she started. "Ben is terribly nervous about what I plan to say today," she said, with glee in her voice. "I told him that I planned to get even with him for all the mischievous pranks he's played in his lifetime." The congregation chuckled. "But I've decided not to do that. I want to share with you instead some of the sweet things he's done — the things that have convinced me that he will make a good missionary."

I was mortified when she began listing things I had done for others from the time I was three-and-a-half years old. She told about the time I gave my brand new boots to Jeffrey Randall, a kid in my fourth-grade class, because he didn't have any. She ended by telling about my love for little children and called it a Christlike quality. She told how little children are always hanging around our house.

"But Ben doesn't like to admit he's a softie," Mom added. "I know he's probably just as red as a beet right now." She was right, I decided, because my face was extremely warm and the congregation was chuckling.

"I think I might have liked it better if Mom had just told about my pranks," I said, still blushing, when I began my speech. Then I tried to sound casual as I continued. But I hadn't done much public speaking, and I was shaking in my shoes. I started slurring, and my voice sounded about as bad as it had the first hour after my coma. I couldn't seem to sound confident, to sound like a smoothie. So I quit trying to be witty and funny and rugged, I pushed my paper aside. Something told me to tell about my conversion.

"Brothers and sisters, as you know, I haven't always been a committed member of the Church. Let's say I was a fun-times Mormon. I was always around for the parties and the ward dinners. Then, as you know, I had my accident. That changed things. During my stay in the hospital, I discovered that the Church is more than fun times. I discovered that life is more than fun times. I discovered that life is a precious gift.

"Now you'll probably look at me and say, 'There's Ben, the fun-time kid.' Well, I'll probably always enjoy having a good time. I'll probably still joke around with you. But in here," I touched my chest, "in here things are different. I love the gospel now. But more than that. I love Jesus Christ, my brother."

At this point my voice cracked a little. "And you know something? Before, when I was joking around, I really wasn't happy. But now . . . now things are different. Now I'm happy on the inside. It's more than happiness. It's a deep, peaceful kind of feeling. And I wouldn't trade it for . . . for . . . well, not for anything earthly."

Then I told how much I loved my family. I said that I hoped

my dad would accept the gospel and that I hoped he was here in spirit. I told how much I loved my mother. I paused. "And I want to tell my sister something," I added. I looked back at Corker. "I want to apologize to her for the hard time I've always given her — for teasing her. See, she was always smarter and faster than I was." They laughed. "She walked when she was only eight months old. Me, I was almost eighteen months. I guess I was waiting for a ride. So I took it out on her, and I punished her. Now I want her to know that I wouldn't trade her for a slower model. I love her and I'm happy that she married Steve, who is one of the greatest guys I've ever known and who was an example to me when I needed one most.

"My sister said something to me when I was just starting out on a running program. I was totally wiped out and I didn't plan to continue. Let's say I was a 'three-hundred-pound weakling.' " I glanced at Darlene, who got a funny look on her face. "But Corker said, 'Ben, a person can do anything.' And I'm here to testify that a person *can* do anything. There's a scripture about that. 'I can do all things through Christ which strengtheneth me.' I know that's true."

Then I thanked them all for coming, and I told them, "I love you all — I really do." With that I returned to my seat. When I looked at the audience again, I noticed a lot of people were sniffing and I saw some blurry eyes and some handkerchiefs being applied, but I was proud of myself. I hadn't lost control. Only once my voice had cracked a little.

I looked down at a beaming Darlene and I winked at her. I hadn't looked at her when I had told everyone that I loved them. I planned to tell her later.

The next evening none of the visitors seemed to notice that Mom had been washing walls and spring cleaning for the huge family night open house. In any case, when everyone had gone home, the place looked a mess. The back yard was getting a little cool, but Darlene and I were still out sitting on lawn chairs. It seemed oddly quiet.

"Well, kid, it's just you, me, and . . ." — I looked around — "a zillion paper cups. I forgot to put out a trash can for people to put them in."

Darlene looked around then too. "I guess we should start picking them up before they blow away, or something."

"Good idea." We began stacking up paper cups.

"Did you know there are a lot of things you can do with paper cups besides drink out of them," I asked, as I balanced one on my nose, barking like a seal and clapping my hands.

Darlene giggled. "And watch this!" I juggled three of them. I did a pretty good job until I stubbed my toe.

"Ouch!" Darlene said, wincing with me.

"Let's see how good our balance is," I suggested, as I placed my stack of cups carefully on my head, held out my arms, and began walking like a tightrope walker. Darlene followed my example, and we found that by cooperating and adding to each other's stacks we could continue picking up the cups.

"This is fun," Darlene said. "Wow, look how high yours is get—" She stopped talking and smiled sheepishly toward our back stoop. "Oh, hi!" she said lifting her hand weakly. I turned my head slowly and saw my mother standing on the stoop with one foot on the top step, her head cocked slightly and her eyebrows lowered. She smiled politely as Darlene tried to explain. "We were just . . . ummm . . . ummm . . ."

"I'm just happy you two are getting things picked up out here," Mom said quickly. "Don't let me disturb you." With another polite smile, she backed toward the door and entered quietly.

Darlene wrinkled her nose at me and winced. "Your mother must think we're crazy," she said, as she removed the stack of cups from her head. "Can you imagine how it must look to see two people walking around with paper cups on their heads. We must have looked like a couple of looney birds."

Darlene had learned the term from me, and I was glad she had used it. "No, I'd say we looked more like twin towers of Babel," I said.

"You look like the Leaning Tower of Pisa right now," Darlene said, smiling. I removed my stack just before it toppled, and picked up a few more cups to add to it.

"Darlene," I said, with mock seriousness. "Did you know that if we put all the paper cups in the house and yard end to end they'd reach California and back?"

"No kidding?" Darlene said. "No, I didn't know that." She was carrying a pile of cups about two feet high.

"Well, did you know . . ." I couldn't think of anything else, and I paused.

"No, I didn't know that either," she giggled.

"Yeah, well, there's a lot you don't know." She was close to me now and I pulled her closer, smashing about fifty paper cups.

"Like what?"

"Like that I—" She put her hand over my mouth.

"Don't say it, Ben."

"Don't say what?" She shrugged and looked up into the sky.

"May I ask you a question?" I mumbled through her fingers.

"Yes." She removed her hand.

"Why do you always put your hand over people's mouths. It's hard to talk. It's a bad habit you have, and I really think you ought to work on it."

"I guess it is." Then she grinned the old Morgan grin, and I turned to whipping cream inside.

"Think you'll be around in two years?" I whispered, talking to her lips.

"I imagine I will be."

"I wish you'd make a point of it," I said, feeling confident that I had been the only name in Darlene's little dating book since my accident. "We've got some marathons to run together. It'll be you and me, kid, running off into the sunset."

She smiled at me, rather tenderly I thought. "I'm very fond of you, Ben," she said. "I . . ."

Say it! Say it! I thought.

"In fact, I'm *extremely* fond of you."

"Oh, yes, well the feeling's mutual," I said. "Believe me, it's mutual."

I leaned down and kissed her.

12

"Canning is the pits," Corker wrote me, after I had been on my mission a short while. It was the first time she had sounded the least bit negative, and her words surprised me.

When I continued her letter, I could see why she was not terribly fond of canning. She had tried to bottle a hundred quarts of peaches on the same day that she had scheduled a dinner party for a few close relatives and friends—*seventeen* close relatives and friends to be exact, including *all* the Morgans. She had decided to go gourmet, and the only thing I recognized on her menu description was lemon jello salad.

She continued:

Things didn't work out as well as I had planned. I only finished sixty bottles. But I'm not giving up. I'm going to stay up all night if I need to, to do the rest of the bottles and to get them all to seal. I think they're supposed to pop, but none of them have so far. Frances offered to help after the party, but I told her I could handle it and I know I can. I just needed to read the instructions again to see what I did wrong. I'm waiting now to see if this batch I've recooked is going to seal. I think I just needed to cook them all longer.

Another thing that set me back is that I kept getting sick to my stomach. I've got a touch of the flu or something, and Steve has talked me into going to the doctor tomorrow.

She must have had some *day,* I thought to myself, and I felt a little sorry for her.

Luckily the party went rather well, thanks to the fact that I really planned ahead carefully. The food wasn't all that bad, thank goodness. I'd hate to have a flop with Frances here for dinner, and I felt it *had* to be good. You know what an excellent cook and hostess she is. Steve helped me with a few of the last-minute details. Why lie? He saved me, and we both worked like crazy the last half-hour trying to clean up the peach mess and get dinner completed. He looked so funny mimicking my frenzy that it made me laugh. He always has a way of helping me relax when I'm taking myself too seriously. He's such a dear man, and I love him so much. He'd be up helping me right now, but he was up all last night with his bookkeeping and I insisted he turn in. I never realized before what a good team we would make. Steve is so willing to help me, and I love helping him too. I'm glad I love him so much, especially right now.

But the tone of her letter changed with the P.S. which she must have added the next day.

The doctor says I'm pregnant. He says my tiredness and nausea are quite normal. I got a little snippy with him and told him that it isn't normal for *me,* and he added that irritability is also typical. How I hate being told I'm typical.

Steve is very happy — elated, in fact. I need to get some books, and I might join the PTA and see what I can find out about schools around here. I don't know much about Jordan School District. I checked into preschools this morning, and I found one or two that I think I'll investigate further. This will be a new experience for Steve and me. Things were going well for us, perfect in fact, but new experiences help us to grow.

It was easy to read between the lines and see that Corker was a little resentful. I could also tell that she was scared. I decided it was time to do a little cheerleading, but I knew I'd need to be subtle about it. I wrote:

So, Corker, it sounds like you had quite a day the other day. Did your lids ever seal? Hope so. It can be discouraging if they don't. Did I ever tell you about the time I tried to bottle apricots? Well, I won't. It was okay until I saw a fruit worm floating in the only bottle that had sealed and I threw the bottle across the kitchen and broke it into smithereens. Believe it or not, I laughed about it later. Frances came over and helped me figure out what I'd done wrong and helped Mom and me clean up the mess. Frances is a real trooper. I hope I don't detect a hint of competition with my good buddy, Frances. Hey, Cork, she's got twenty-five years experience on you! We're all climbing different ladders and we can all help each other — right? Speaking of ladders, quit trying to skip rungs. You're just lucky you didn't fall on your face. "Line upon line, precept on precept" — remember?

And about this kid you and Steve are going to have. You know what I think? I think that's about the greatest news I've heard. Man, what a kid that will be! While you're checking out colleges for him (or her), why don't you find out where I can join the Future Uncles of America Society.

When I reread the letter, I could tell I hadn't been as subtle as I had planned to be, but I folded it up and sent it off anyway. I figured that Corker knew by now that subtlety wasn't my middle name.

I was gratified when the next letter from Corker was positive again. She had completed her canning marathon and had bottled a couple of hundred bottles of peaches, plums, apples, and even grapes for grape juice. "They're absolutely beautiful," she said. I assumed they had all sealed. "Now I'm moving on to breads," she added. "Now, *bread* is the real challenge, as far as I'm concerned."

"Ben, you're right," she continued. "I need to take my rungs one step at a time, especially now that I'm expecting. It's always been hard for me to do that." Then she listed "a few" of the books on child-rearing she had read, some of them while waiting in the doctor's office. There were about ten on the list.

She said she and Steve were getting excited about things such as politics and law. Steve had decided to go into law, she thought. "What we've studied together is fascinating. I'd like to investigate the possibility of going into law myself someday, but right now I'm thinking family, family, family, family!"

Quite a few letters later, when I was well into my mission, Corker told me she had switched her teaching classes from aerobic dance to self-esteem.

As you know, Ben, Steve and I have always enjoyed attending those lectures and seminars, and we've both done a lot of reading in the psycho-cybernetics area, and I've done quite a bit of personal research. Now that I'm too big to teach dance, self-esteem is a natural. But mainly I'm teaching it because the ladies want it so badly. Frances registered, and we're working out a trade. She's going to teach me advanced bread-making and cooking in her home. I could never figure out how long to knead the bread to get it to the right consistency, or how warm to warm the yeast. There's only so much you can learn from books. I decided I might as well learn from the best, and Frances, I admit, *is* the best.

Frankly, I couldn't understand why she would need to take self-esteem, but it touched me that she was interested. Then, just before our first session, she confided in me that she didn't think she had any talents. "All I've ever done is keep house," she said.

"Oh, but Frances, you're an artist," I said. "You have a real talent, believe me!" I told her how she amazed me. I also told her how much I admire her and love her, because I do.

Ben, you can't believe all the sharp ladies who are signing up because they feel they need more self-esteem. I have a waiting list two pages long, and I just started the class. I'm just excited that in some small way I might have a chance to help.

I smiled, sighed, and put Corker's letter down. Then I picked up Darlene's recent letter and reread it. It was still the same letter, filled with inspirational quotes, interesting happenings, and a few lines from little Josh. The letter smelled as sweet as she was, and I put it to my nostrils and breathed deeply. Then I put it away. Elder Simmons, my companion, and I had work to do. We had six discussions left to teach that day, and if we wanted to keep up our teaching pace we had several more firsts to set. "Let's get going, Elder," I said.

"You're talking my language," he answered. I liked Elder Simmons. We really *did* talk the same language. He was a cool man with a bone-crushing handshake. We had been working together only a little over two weeks, and we were already good buddies.

That night, after we had had our prayers, we started talking about the work and then we talked a little about our families. I mentioned Corker, and Elder Simmons commented on her name.

"It's a nickname," I explained. "It means a remarkable person. There are other definitions, but that's the one that applies to her. You've probably met the type—the kind of person who runs circles around other people and makes them nervous. You know, one of those nonstop types."

"Sure, I've met the type." He grinned. "Sounds to me like she takes after Big Brother."

I shook my head. "No, Corker is a real speedy. I've always been slower than Heinz catsup."

"Aw, come on! You don't need to play humble with me, so cut it out."

I gave him a funny look. "Huh?"

He laughed. "I said, 'cut it out.' You must know you're a corker. You think we didn't hear about the time you turned one referral into a four-family baptism session?"

"Oh, yeah," I said, smiling and nodding. "That was quite a deal."

"And that time you spoke on a panel in some church group meeting and you taught fifteen of the people and they all joined the Church."

"You heard about that too, huh?"

"Who hasn't? Everyone in the mission knows who you are, Elder, old buddy."

"No kidding?" I wanted to ask him if he had heard anything else.

When he didn't continue, I decided to be helpful. "Then there's my leadership record."

"Oh, yes, that's right. What, zone leader in five months?"

"Right! That's not too bad. Actually, it was four-and-a-half months."

"Oh," he said slowly, thoughtfully.

"And I guess I nearly doubled the record number of baptisms made by a missionary. I guess I've set a new pace for this mission."

"True," he said slowly, as I nodded vigorously. I was thinking about how I had not only climbed the ladder of success, but I had actually jumped off to fly through the sky on wings that I didn't even know I had. He was right. I giggled.

"I guess I *am*."

"What?"

"You're right. I *am* a corker. I hadn't realized it before, but it's true."

Elder Simmons looked at me sideways. "Yeah, well, don't let it go to your head."

I laughed heartily. "I won't," I assured him, as I slapped him on the back with a little too much gusto. "Don't worry, I won't."

But the more I thought about my successes and about what the missionaries said about me, the more I felt that I should exercise my talents in the highest leadership position an Elder can reach in the mission field. I knew that Elder Jensen was going home soon, and that would open up the position of assistant to the president. Clearly I deserved the position, and clearly I could do a better job as the president's assistant than any other Elder in the mission. And because he knew my record, the mission president would draw the only possible conclusion: I was the man for the job.

Every day I looked expectantly for a letter from the president.

Finally the president phoned and said he wanted to talk to me in person in his office. I acted naive, but I felt assured about what he wanted. The next day I walked into his office with a confident smile on my face.

But President Rollings didn't smile back. He pushed his glasses up on his nose and cleared his throat. "Have a seat, Elder Van Vleet," he said courteously. Then he leaned forward and looked me in the eye. "You've probably heard that Elder Jensen is going home soon."

"Yes," I said, trying not to sound too eager.

"To tell you the truth, you were the first one I considered for the position. I was sure you were to be our next assistant, but when I prayed about it, I got a different answer. I received inspiration that you're needed for something else."

"Oh!" My stomach must have fallen to the floor, because I couldn't feel anything inside of me but an empty pit. I didn't speak at first.

"We have a big group of new Elders here, and you and several others are needed to train them. We need the strongest, most motivated Elders we have to pass on that enthusiasm and expertise."

"Anything you think is best, President," I said numbly.

"So let's get out there and meet them." He stood up and I stood up. "I knew you'd understand," he said, shaking my hand firmly. "I feel good about you, Elder Van Vleet. And I know you've got what it takes."

I walked out of the president's office feeling sure I had been demoted in spite of his "Go-get-em" speech. "Come with me," he said. "I want you to meet Elder Squigley."

Several large, burly Elders shook my hand as they waited for their new companions. Then President Rollings introduced me to Elder Squigley. *I knew it,* I thought to myself. *My luck's run out.*

"Hello," Elder Squigley squeaked, and he held out a small frail hand.

"Elder," I said politely. "I'm Elder Van Vleet. These your suitcases?" I hoped the president couldn't hear the disappointment in my voice.

"Let me take them for you," I said. *Since it doesn't look like you could handle them yourself,* I added to myself. I was tempted to put Elder Squigley under one arm and his luggage under the other and carry them out. I knew I would probably have gotten a good laugh, from some of the Elders, but I also knew the president wasn't too keen on that kind of humor.

As we walked out to my car, the car I wouldn't have for much longer, Elder Squigley played the typical role of the new Elder and followed me so closely that when I stopped he bumped into me. He continued this behavior for the next few weeks. "Heel!" I felt like saying, as he followed me like a well-trained show dog. "Elder," I finally said. "I don't think you need to take that mission rule quite so literally. We are supposed to stick with our companions, but I need a little breathing room, okay? How about another foot or so?"

"Oh sure, sorry," he squeaked.

This guy is not cool. He is not tough, and he is definitely not with it, I said to myself often. *Why me?* I wondered. I also wondered how long I would have him to train.

I don't think just my new training assignment alone would have started me soaring downward if at about the same time I hadn't gotten another setback—a major setback. I suppose I had known subconsciously that it would come, but I had never admitted it to myself.

Darlene's easy flowing handwriting started out with the words "Dear Ben," but they might as well have been "Dear John." The letter told in a careful, sweet way that she had met someone else and that she had given it careful thought and prayer and she knew that he was the person she wanted to spend eternity with. She hoped I would not let it affect my mission. She would always cherish our friendship. I wondered if there was a "Dear John" form letter somewhere that girls use. The only thing original was the last line, which read: "I guess we won't be running in those marathons together, but I know you'll find someone else to run with."

I read the letter twice, folded it carefully, and put it back in the envelope.

Elder Squigley seemed to sense my misery at once. "You okay, Elder? You look sick."

"I'm fine."

"Are you sure? You look like you just got a 'Dear John' or something."

"Yup," I said. "I sure did! Life's tough, isn't it?"

I needed to be alone. I started out of the front door of our apartment, but Elder Squigley stood up quickly and tried to go with me. We got stuck in the doorway. "Do you mind, Elder," I said rather sharply. "For just this once could I be more than a foot away from you?" The last thing I needed right then was to have him breathing down my neck. "I'm just going out to sit on the stoop. If you want you can frisk me for sharp objects. And I'll tell you what. You can sit by the window and check on me every few seconds, okay?"

He seemed to feel that was a satisfactory solution, and he sat in the window well where he could easily open the curtains and peek out of them to check on me.

It was dark outside, and the stars flickered clearly at me. I took the letter out of the envelope again, reopened it, and read it again by the porch light. I guess I was hoping that this time the words would be different. But they weren't and I sat back down and laid the letter on my knee. I looked up at the Big Dipper.

Oh great! I thought. *That's all I need, to have old Squeaky see me out here crying. Good show!*

I wiped my eyes on my arm and got control of myself quickly. *What am I so upset about, anyway?* I asked myself. *If I'd been smart I would have seen it coming.* I looked straight ahead at the street light. *But then I was never known for being smart.*

The thought came to me of my mission "theme song": A person can do anything . . . get anything, if he's willing to work for it. *Ha!* I thought. I knew I had worked for Darlene. There was no doubt about that. I had worked for her, all right. I had sweated for her. I had starved for her. I had lost sixty pounds for her. I had even shaved off my moustache for her.

I put my head in my hand. I had loved Darlene. And where had it gotten me? Nowhere. *Life is the pits,* I told myself. *There's no fairness.* I remembered my accident, and I wondered why it had happened. *Why?* I asked myself. *Why do I always get smacked down just when I start feeling great? First I get zapped by a yellow truck, and then by a nineteen-year-old skinny girl. And I really worked for her,* I repeated.

As I sat there, it hit me. Darlene wasn't a thing that I could work for. She was a person with her own mind and her own free agency. Maybe a person can earn anything he wants in this life, but he can't *get* anyone. The fact was simple. Darlene hadn't wanted me. It was becoming clear now. She had never treated me as anything but a friend until the accident, and then . . . then she had just pitied me. *You dummy!* I thought. *You made a fool of yourself. If you had had any sense you would have been able to figure it out. She never, never felt the same about you.*

I rolled my head back. What made me think I was worth anything anyway? What made me think I was worth loving? I recalled that I had never done well in school. I began remembering the old Ben, who was a physical and spiritual weakling;

the slow Ben, who couldn't even beat his baby sister to a diploma. And I started feeling bitterness. Corker . . . Corker was married now, and soon she would have a family — kids. She had someone who worshipped the ground she walked on. Somebody loved her. Me, I was sitting on the stoop of a rundown apartment with a "Dear John" in my hand and a missionary companion staring at me out of the window — a guy who didn't trust me further than two feet away from him. I felt like a jerk — a big dumb jerk.

I sat on the stoop for quite a while folding and unfolding the letter before I went back into what we called an apartment. We had rented it furnished, but the only thing that was worth anything inside was a small TV. We had never bothered to tell the landlord that we didn't need it. We had merely unplugged it. Now I plugged it back in and sat down on the sofa in front of it. Elder Squigley stared at me. "Are you going to watch that?"

"Yup."

"But, Elder —"

"Look, I don't care right now, okay?"

"But you won't be able to get up for —"

"Go to bed, Elder," I said. "Go to bed, okay?"

The next morning I had a TV hangover. I had watched the late movie and then the late-late movie. After the TV had gone off the air, I finally zonked out. About eight-thirty I began waking up. I could see Elder Squigley sitting at the kitchen table, studying diligently. Then I saw the letter on the coffee table, and I remembered why I was lying on the couch in my clothes. *Darlene!* My stomach jerked, and I felt like lying back down. "Good morning," Elder Squigley called cheerfully.

I didn't answer but stumbled to the bathroom instead. I tried to awaken myself with some cold water, but when I came out I was not a new man. I still felt rotten. I walked to the fridge, remembering that misery is the best time to eat. I was also remembering that a kind sister in one of the wards had brought over two pies and we hadn't finished them. By nine-thirty I had eaten everything in the fridge except the mayonnaise, and I had watched two quiz programs.

"Elder, it's nine-thirty," Elder Squigley reminded me gently, with just a hint of a squeak in his voice. "Don't you think we'd better . . ."

I leaned across the couch to a corner table and pulled a telephone directory out of the drawer. "Let's do a little telephone tracting," I said, handing him the book. "It will be a good experience for you." I told him in general terms what he should say and he listened carefully, then went right to work. He checked the names off with precision and made notations in the margins.

The chances of setting a first discussion by telephone tracting are about one in thirty-five. Elder Squigley glued himself to the phone but finally put it down and jumped up from his chair. He was excited. "I just set a first discussion!" he said.

"Oh," I mumbled. "Well, isn't that great! When?"

He looked at his watch. "In just an hour."

"An hour?" I sat up unhappily.

"Oh, no!" he said. "And my bike. . . . We were going to take my bike in first thing this morning. Well" . . . He pulled out a bus schedule that I didn't even know he had. "Okay," he said as he began outlining some detailed plans. "Can you be ready in fifteen minutes, Elder?"

"No," I said lying back down.

"Well, you'll have to be ready in fifteen minutes because I've got it all outlined."

I didn't move.

"Elder! Come on, move it!" he said with a squeak. I stared up at him.

"Okay. Okay, if you say so." I obediently hurried to the bathroom.

Fifteen minutes later, on the way out the door, Elder Squigley presented me with my mail. It had come early. I glanced through it, recognized my sister's feminine but businesslike handwriting, and put the letter in my scriptures. I didn't feel like hearing all about her amazing accomplishments right now.

Elder Squigley did a pretty good job on the first discussion. The people weren't golden, but they weren't ungolden either. It wasn't until we were on our way home on the bus that I remembered the letter from Corker. I figured there was nothing better to do, so I tore it open.

"Dear Ben," it began. The next part was written like a telegram in large print: "BABY BOY: TEN POUNDS, THREE OUNCES, BORN THREE-THIRTY-TWO, APRIL 14."

I found myself smiling. The letter continued telling how she had gone into labor in the middle of a positive thinking seminar. She'd had to have Steve help her climb the stairs in the Salt Palace as four or five thousand people watched.

I continued reading through the letter eagerly, looking for something. I didn't even know what I was looking for, but then I found it.

Ben, at first I didn't know if I loved him. It was awful. But delivery had been difficult, and when the doctor asked me if I wanted to hold him I really didn't want to. I was mad at the little tyke for giving me such a bad time. I let Steve hold him, and I watched them together. You've never seen such a proud father. I felt happy inside because Steve was happy.

A few hours later, after I had had some time to recover a little, they brought him to me and I looked at him lying asleep. I looked at his little hands, no, they're big — big for a newborn. Anyway, they were clenched into tiny fists, and his little mouth was sucking at the air. His face was still puffy, but I could already tell he was going to have Steve's nose and my ears. I just kept looking at him until I realized the most wonderful thing: I loved him. All on my own, without Steve's help, I loved him. I loved that little kid with all my being. It was wonderful.

Later Steve came for a special dinner the hospital has that dads can come to, and he picked up the baby, and I looked at them together and I thought *How could I ever have wanted anything else?* I realized then that Steve and I are partners with God in the greatest corporation imaginable: parenthood. We had participated in the process of giving life. I can't think of anything more exciting or important. And rich? I'm the richest woman in the world. Ben, I really can't describe the feeling I had at that moment or the feelings I have had since.

I put the letter down for a minute and stretched my eyes and swallowed. Elder Squigley touched my arm with compassion. "Another 'Dear John,' Elder?"

"No," I said, with a squeak in my voice. "It's my sister. She just had a baby and . . . and she loves him."

"Oh, I see." Elder Squigley nodded and tried to look understanding. "And . . . and is that unusual?"

I smiled. "I'll have to tell you about Corker some time." I picked the letter back up and continued reading. At last I came to the P.S. "Ben," it said, "we would like very much to name the baby after a great king we know. A winner named Benjamin: *you*. That is, if it's all right."

I had been able to control myself up to that point, but now my heart began pouring out of my eyes freely. It was a funny feeling, because passengers were staring at me, and soon others joined them, but it didn't matter. I didn't need to be tough right now. The tears kept flowing down my face. Elder Squigley asked, "Are you okay?"

"I sure am, Elder," I answered. I looked him in the eye for the first time since we had become companions. He had strong clear eyes that didn't flinch when you looked into them. "I'm fine, now," I said.

Then I grinned. "By the way you did a super job on that discussion. I forgot to tell you. You did one whale of a good job. You surprised me, Elder." He beamed at me.

I looked out of the bus window at the sky and I felt like flying again. I could feel that my wings were back. I began looking around the bus at the people. I loved them. I loved every one of them and I wanted to share the gospel with them.

"Elder Squigley," I asked. "How many people in this bus do you think would like to hear about the restored gospel?"

"If they understood it, all of them," he answered.

"How would you like it if you and I set some first discussions right now."

"Right now? Right here on the bus?"

I nodded.

"That's what we're here for," he answered, and I liked his answer.

Elder Squigley rose to his feet as he asked, "Which side do you want?"